Way to go

Strategic approach to English learning

以**教育部**大學英語能力指標2至6級為根據，對照歐盟英語能力指標(CEF)為A2至B1。

一本由臺灣人寫給臺灣學生看的

英文│教材

黃聖慧—總編審　陳憶如、蔡佳蓉—著

五大特色：

1. 囊括「聽、說、讀、寫」四種語言學習方式。
2. 以教育部大學英語能力指標2至6級為根據，對照歐盟英語能力指標(CEF)為A2至B1。
3. 文法編寫以多益英語能力測驗(TOEIC)文法範圍為基礎，由易而難編排。
4. 可作為大學及技職院校基本英文教材，亦或作為一般學生自修的英文教材。
5. 真正從**在地生活**出發；加上英文師培老師的親自撰寫，
   讓你在**地學習、成長、語文能力All Pass！**

序

　　英語學習經常讓許多學子感覺難過與無力。最常聽到的困擾不外：「單字背不起來」，「閱讀能力太差」，「聽力抓不到重點」，「口說不流暢」，「文法公式不會應用」，「寫作不知如何下手」。對於英語的恐懼與學習上的挫折往往讓學生們喪失學習的動機以及勇氣。

　　本書針對學生面臨的常見問題，以教育部大學英語能力指標 2 至 6 級為根據，對照歐盟英語能力指標為 A2 至 B1，循序漸進。每個單元包括單字、閱讀、文法、聽力、口說、寫作以及特殊目的英文（ESP）等七大項目。每個項目融入英語學習策略，以幫助學生更有效率地完成每種技能的學習，進而鍛鍊其往後英語學習上的自主能力。

　　綜觀當前英語學習教科書，少數為大學及技術校院大一英文學習目標專編的教科書，而將學習各種英語技能方法融合於各單元中呈現的亦不多見。藉由本書的編輯脈絡，教師可以比較輕鬆地將學生的程度提升至既定目標；而學生可望學習到各種學習方法與英語技能，以奠定良好的英文發展基礎。

黃聖慧

彰化師範大學英語系暨英語研究所教授

本書特色

1. 本書以教育部大學英語能力指標 2 至 6 級為根據，對照歐盟英語能力指標（CEF）為 A2 至 B1。

2. 本書以一般目的英文（EGP）為主，每一單元結合特殊目的英文（ESP），並以內容為軸心架構（content-based）呈現。每單元包括單字、閱讀、文法、聽力、口說、寫作及特殊目的英文等七大項目。

3. 一般目的英文主題以生活及就業之實用性為編寫原則，內容包括食、衣、住、行、娛樂、社交禮儀等。

4. 特殊目的英文範圍以大專院校科系為主，含括視傳、餐飲管理、旅遊、生物、醫療保健、金融、設計、語言、運動、教育等領域。

5. 每單元運用本文內容，提供聽、說、讀、寫、單字等學習策略之範例及練習。

6. 本書文法編寫以多益英語能力測驗（TOEIC）文法範圍為基礎，由易而難編排。

7. 各單元之文法與學習策略運用以中文編寫，讓學習無障礙。

8. 本書可作為大學及技職院校基本英文教材，亦或作為大學先修教材。

本書用法

給老師 ——

1. 根據教育部大學英語能力指標研究，一般大學畢業生應具備 8 級以上之英語能力（教育部大學英語能力指標分為 1 至 12 級）。本書以教育部大學英語能力指標 2 至 6 級為根據，對照歐盟英語能力指標為 A2 至 B1。

2. 本書為全方位之英語學習教材，每單元包括單字、閱讀、文法、聽力、口說、寫作及特殊目的英文（ESP）等七大項目，可供教師根據課程需求選擇利用。

3. 本書特殊目的英文（ESP）範圍涵蓋視傳、餐飲管理、旅遊、生物、醫療保健、金融、設計、語言、運動、教育等，教師可根據學生之主副修領域及興趣選擇教授。

4. 為發展學生之學習能力，每單元結合本文內容，提供各類聽、說、讀、寫、單字學習策略之範例及練習，可作為老師示範學習策略的方法與步驟。

5. 第一到第八單元以單字為開端，提供接下來聽、說、讀、寫練習的基礎；第九到第十六單元以閱讀為開端，讓學習者透過上下文來學習這些單元所涵蓋的單字。

6. 本書閱讀編排由表格、段落至全篇文章，由短而長，由易而難，循序漸進，以利教師之使用。

7. 各單元皆提供單字表作為教學之整理。

給學生 ——

1. 本書提供各類學習策略，包含聽、說、讀、寫、單字記憶等策略講解，搭配策略練習，學生可使用這些策略於各種不同的情境中，讓英語學習更有趣、更有效率。

2. 本書依單字難易度及閱讀篇幅長短的方式編排，學生可以累積單字量，並且透過閱讀熟習各領域的知識。

3. 本書所附贈的試題可作為學生學習成效之評量。

4. 各單元提供單字表可作為復習之使用。

Contents

序 / 本書特色 / 本書用法

Skills Unit	Reading	Grammar	Writing	Speaking
1. Movie (p.1)	Movie reviews	A, an, the	Writing an outline of a story	Practicing linking sounds
2. Hotel (p.11)	Hotel rooms	Review: futureUse of "would prefer"	"would prefer" sentence writing practice	Practicing the contraction "I'd"
3. Food (p.21)	Restaurant advertisements	Comparisons with adjectives	Writing sentences to compare restaurants	Expressing preference
4. Travel & Flight (p.33)	Flight itinerary	Indirect questions	Completing forms	Asking about places
5. Clothes (p.43)	Clothes labels	Passive voice	Writing instructions	Discussing what to buy
6. Health (p.53)	Clinic Notice	Modal auxiliaries	Writing a paragraph to provide some advice	Telephone conversation and leaving messages
7. Living Green (p.63)	Saving the earth and your money	Countable & uncountable nouns Review: Present simple & continuous	Keeping a journal	Talking about what you do to go green

AND PLAN

Listening	ESP	Strategies
Famous movies – agreeing/ disagreeing	Film editing	1. 單字分類法 2. 瀏覽閱讀法 3. 擬出寫作大綱 4. 辨別說話語調
Hotel room booking	Working as a hotel receptionist	1. 看字讀音 2. 掃描閱讀法 3. 聽特定訊息
A conversation in a restaurant	Working as a waiter or waitress	1. 音譯相近法 2. 單字分類法 3. 掃描閱讀法 4. 模仿連音 5. 利用關鍵字猜測
Announcements	Being a tourist guide – introducing places	1. 故事串連記憶法 2. 圖表瀏覽 3. 聽關鍵字
A conversation in a clothes shop	Working as a clerk in a department store	1. 單字分類法 2. 圖片猜測法 3. 數字練習 4. 做筆記
Telephone conversation	Working as a nurse in a clinic	1. 拆字法 2. 故事串聯法 3. 圖表瀏覽 4. 做筆記
A short talk about energy saving	Renewable energy	1. 拆字法 2. 透過第一段文章理解 3. 如何寫日誌 4. 聽說話的技巧

Unit \ Skills	Reading	Grammar	Writing	Speaking
8. Banking (p.79)	How to save your money	Subjunctive verbs	Writing opinions about how to save money	Expressions opinions
9. Common Courtesy (p.91)	How to have common courtesy	Using gerund as a noun phrase	Writing a story and comments	Giving compliments
10. Housing (p.103)	How to decorate my living room	Preposition	Writing a composition describing a picture	Describing location
11. Technology (p.117)	The development of technology	Past simple & present perfect	Writing a paragraph	Talking about inventions
12. Novel & Music (p.131)	Story - The man and his donkey	Causative verbs	Writing a short story	Solving problems
13. Biology (p.143)	Blood types and personalities	2nd conditional – "If- clause"	Writing a paragraph	Talking about unreal present situations
14. Fashion Design (p.153)	Johan Ku, another "Glory of Taiwan"	3rd conditional – "If- clause"	Writing a paragraph	Talking about unreal past situations
15. Sport (p.163)	Statistics of sports injury	Infinitive	Using outline to compose an article	Introducing a sport
16. Education (p.177)	Educational systems of Japan and the US	Contrast signals	Using outline to compose an article	Expressing your preference

Student Book Answer Keys   p.189

Listening	ESP	Strategies
A short talk about credit card	Working as a bank receptionist	1. 字首字尾法 2. 同義反義法 3. 標題預測 4. 利用片語爭取思考時間 5. 聽表達順序的字詞
A short talk about courteous behavior	Working as a sales representatives	1. 瀏覽閱讀法 2. 字首字尾法 3. 聽關鍵字及做筆記
Descriptions of four rooms	Interior design	1. 單字猜測技巧 2. 拆字法 3. 列下寫作要點 4. 空間描述 5. 圖片預測技巧 6. 掃瞄閱讀法
A short talk about facebook	My phone 5 specifications	1. 掃瞄閱讀法 2. 寫文章大意 3. 利用字的變化形 4. 聽指引或是表達順序的字詞
Song - Are you lonesome tonight?	"Real" Languages in the Lord of the Rings	1. 利用故事分析圖 2. 圖像記憶法 3. 聽連音
Guessing people's blood types	Health food specifications	1. 依上下文猜字 2. 字首記憶法 3. 聽關鍵字
An interview with a famous fashion designer	Hair style & make-up	1. 瀏覽閱讀法 2. 個人化 3. 聽懂問題
Two instructions about swimming	How to avoid injuries in sports	1. 掃瞄閱讀法 2. 單字分類法 3. 擷取重點
Two lectures about education	Working as a children's English teacher in a cram school	1. 生字猜測技巧 2. 拆字法 3. 結構性複習法 4. 條列口說要點 5. 善用承轉語詞 6. 擷取重點

Unit

1

Movie

Warm up

A. Have you ever watched the movie "Up"? Do you like it? How much do you know about it? What is your favorite movie? Why?

B. Do you know how a movie is made? Number the pictures from 1 to 6.

☐ design the costume

☐ write out the script

☐ edit the film

☐ choose the cast

☐ shoot the film

☐ add the sound effects

Vocabulary

💡單字策略——單字分類法

背單字的時候我們可以把單字分門別類來幫助記憶。例如：actor（男演員）及 actress（女演員）就屬於 cast（卡司陣容）。

試著將下列單字依其屬性分類吧！

actor	director	cameraman	actress	screenwriter	character
film editor	scene	screenplay	lighting designer	sound editor	

Cast	Script	Film shooting	Film editing
actor *actress*			

單字表

1. costume ['kɑstjum]	(n)服裝、戲裝	例	She puts on the costume for the play.
2. script [skrɪpt]	(n)（戲劇、廣播等的）腳本、底稿	例	Good presenters do not read their scripts while presenting.
3. cast [kæst]	(n)班底、演員陣容	例	The movie is famous for its strong cast.
4. shoot [ʃut]	(v)拍攝 (n)拍攝	例	This film was shot in Taipei. Join us for a group photo shoot.
5. effect [ɪ'fɛkt]	(n)（色彩、聲音等產生的）印象；效果	例	New technology can improve the effects of photos.
6. director [də'rɛktɚ]	(n)（電影等的）導演	例	Ang Lee is a famous director from Taiwan.
7. cameraman ['kæmərə,mæn]	(n)（電視、電影等的）攝影師；攝影記者	例	I've always dreamed of becoming a cameraman.
8. screenwriter ['skrin,raɪtɚ]	(n)劇本作家；編劇家	例	A screenwriter writes stories.
9. character ['kærəktɚ]	(n)（小說、戲劇等的）人物、角色	例	My favorite character in the movie "Up" is Russell.
10. scene [sin]	(n)場景；（電影、電視的）一個鏡頭	例	The scene is so beautiful.

11. lighting ['laɪtɪŋ]	(n)照明、舞臺燈光	例	The lighting is very important for a horror film.
12. screenplay ['skrin,ple]	(n)電影劇本	例	A screenplay is written by a screenwriter.

Reading

💡閱讀策略——瀏覽閱讀法

　　閱讀英文就像閱讀中文一般，除了特殊目的外，我們並不常一字一句地去研究琢磨。相反地，我們是快速地瀏覽閱讀，並透過我們所懂的單字來理解或推測作者想要表達的意思。現在就用這個方法快速瀏覽閱讀接下來 Part A 的文章。你能夠理解作者想要表達的意見嗎？請在下面的空格中寫下你的答案，並寫下幫助你理解的字或詞。

A. Reading movie reviews.

1. **Skim the movie review below. What does John think of the movie "Up"?**

Great movie	November 9, 2009 By John

 I really like the screenplay. Without a doubt, it is funny. I really love the story. I feel that "Up" shows a very nice and touching story. The old man's love for his wife and the kid's dream can't be forgotten. And the scenes are so colorful and beautiful. I have watched the movie not only once, but more than five times. I feel "Up" is a great movie. Thanks a lot to the director and all the people who worked behind the scenes.

John thinks:

Words and phrases that help me understand this movie review:

2. **Share your answers with your classmates. What helps you understand the whole passage?**

B. More practice. Read two more movie reviews. What do these people think about the movie "Up"? Write the answers and the words/phrases that help you understand the reviews.

UP, up?	June 1, 2009 By Nina

 I think the movie is unrealistic. Those two old characters are not like ordinary old people. See their actions? They were like action stars. And I don't really like those super dogs. I'd prefer something more realistic. The ending is not as surprising as I would have expected. I wonder why the screenwriter didn't make the ending funnier. The scenes could also be done better. I prefer other Pixar movies.

Nina thinks:

Words and phrases that help me understand this movie review:

UP is the top	May 28, 2009 By Lillian

 "This movie is now my favorite Pixar movie. Although I'd prefer to see Ellie alive, the characters and the story are already superb. I especially love Dug, the dog who wanted Mr. Frederickson to be his master. He's my favorite character in the movie. There are so many parts that I like about the movie. Taking the sound effects for example, the sound editor must have done a lot because the sound effects really surprised me. Everybody should go and see it.

Lillian thinks:

Words and phrases that help me understand this movie review:

Grammar

A. 你知道什麼時候使用 **a / an** 以及 **the** 嗎？

a / an	非特定的單數可數名詞	There is **a** shoe on the ground.
	工作名稱	Beth is **a** teacher
the	特定的人、事、物	**The** book I read was borrowed from **the** library near my house
	特定的國籍的人	**the** Chinese / **the** Americans
	人、事、物的種類	**the** rich / **the** poor
	稱謂	**the** king / **the** queen
	最高級形容詞	**the** smartest boy / **the** best student
	唯一的事物	**the** sun / **the** moon / **the** earth
	集合或複數的國家名稱	**the** USA / **the** Philippines
	河流、山脈、海名	**the** Nile / **The** Rhine **the** Alpines / **the** Himalayas **the** Pacific / **the** Atlantic
無冠詞	普遍的人、事、物或複數可數名詞	Shops are closed early on Sundays.
	單數國家名稱	Taiwan / France / Japan
	街道名、地名	Wall Street / Taipei

B. 在下列空格中填入 **a / an, the**，或打叉（✕）。

When there is _____ Hollywood, there is _____ Bollywood. _____ Bollywood is the name used for _____ film industry in _____ India, _____ country near _____ Indian Ocean. _____ Bollywood is _____ largest film producer in India and one of _____ largest centers of film production in _____ world. _____ Bollywood movies are mostly musicals. They are often presented with _____ songs and dance. _____ film's success often depends on the quality of _____ songs and dance. _____ film's music is often released before the movie itself and helps get more people to know about it.

Writing

A. Can you write about one of your favorite movies?

💡寫作策略——擬出寫作大綱

　　當我們寫作的時候並不是拿起筆來就一直寫。我們應該先計劃想要寫的內容，把它的大概勾勒出來，也就是我們所說的大綱（outline），再根據大綱來寫作。常見的大綱型式有下列兩種：

1. bullet points / numbers（列點式）

　　(1)Background of the story

　　　① What is the movie?

　　　② Where did things happen?

　　(2)Middle of the story

　　　① What happened?

　　(3)End of the story

　　　① What is the ending?

　　　② What do I think about it?

2. flaw chart（流程圖式）

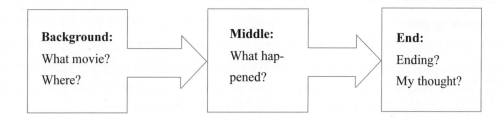

現在就選擇其中一種方式，在下面的空格裡寫下你最喜歡的電影大綱。

Speaking

🎵 **Track 1**

A. **Listen and practice saying the sounds out loud.**

a [ə] or [æ]

an [ən] or [æn]

the [ðə] or [ðɪ]

🎵 **Track 2**

B. **Practice reading the sentences out loud. Mark the linking sounds.**

1. An apple a day keeps the doctor away.

2. The house around the corner is new.

3. Beauty is in the eye of the beholder.

4. Life is like a ladder, the higher you climb, the more expansive your view is.

🎵 **Track 3**

C. **Listen and check if the linking sounds you marked are correct. Then practice reading the sentences aloud with your partner.**

Listening

🎧 **Track 4**

A. Listen to people talking about the famous movie - Avatar. Do they agree or disagree with each other that Avatar is a good movie? Why? Circle the correct answer and write down the reason.

> **Avatar**
>
> | **Agree** | **Disagree** |
> |---|---|
>
> Reason:

💡**聽力策略─辨別說話語調**

　　當我們聽他人談論對於某人、事或物的看法時，我們不但可以從他們說話的內容來了解他們的觀點，還可以從說話者的語氣聽出他們對於同一人、事或物的立場。語氣是非常重要的。同一句話 "Oh, yeah!" 當你以不同語氣表達時，聽話者的理解是不同的。例如：當說話者同意彼此看法時，語氣通常是較興奮的也較急促。而當說話者不同意彼此的看法時，語氣通常是低沉而且較慢的。例如：當對話中的男生說 "Oh, yeah" 時，他的語氣較沉，聽起來就是對於這部電影不感到興奮。相對於這個女生說話語氣的提高，我們可以推測兩人對於這部電影的看法是不一樣的。

　　此外，要了解說話者立場就要注意肯定及否定的用詞，例如：agree, like, love 等就是肯定的詞，至於 disagree, not（例如：don't, isn't）, but 等就是否定的詞。

🎧 **Track 5**

B. Listen to people talking about one more movie. Do they agree or disagree with each other? Why? Circle the correct answer and write down the reason.

> **The Twilight Saga: New moon**
>
> | **Agree** | **Disagree** |
> |---|---|
>
> Reason:

ESP

Film editing is part of the after filming process. It involves the selection and combining of shots. It is an art of storytelling. A film editor does not simply cut off or edit scenes. He / She has to work creatively with images, story, dialogue, music, and the actors' performances.

A. These are terms used in film editing. Match the word with its correct meaning.

a. establishing shot   **d.** fade in/out   **g.** insert shot   **j.** cross cutting

b. freeze-frame   **e.** final cut   **h.** eyeline match

c. editing   **f.** cut away   **i.** dissolve

_____ 1. 剪輯

_____ 2. 交叉剪接（把兩個發生在不同地點的鏡頭接在一起，暗示它們是同時發生的，或是用來做對比的）

_____ 3. 視線搭配（指主角與其所視物體在兩個鏡頭中的搭配）

_____ 4. 建立鏡頭（通常是一個遠景，讓觀眾知道接下來的故事的所在地點）

_____ 5. 停格

_____ 6. 切出鏡頭（加入相關卻非必要的鏡頭，將觀眾的注意力由主戲引開）

_____ 7. 精剪（電影放映的完成版本）

_____ 8. 溶接（將一鏡頭的結尾與另一鏡頭的開始重疊在一起，漸漸地轉鏡至另一場景）

_____ 9. 淡入／淡出

_____ 10. 插入鏡頭

Unit  2

Hotel

Warm up

A. Match the words with the pictures. Then find out which one is the extra word. Do you know what this word means?

1.

2.

3.

a. to book
b. a double room
c. a twin room
d. a front desk
e. to greet
f. a pet
g. a suite
h. an inn

4.

5.

6.

7.

Did you find the extra word? What is the meaning of this word? _____

Vocabulary

💡單字策略——練習看字讀音

　　在英語拼字上，不同的字母排列方式，會產生不同的發音，而這大多是有規則可尋的。而這個規則可以幫助我們讓拚字更加容易。

規則一 在只有一個短母音的英文字中或只有一個母音的重音節中，字母 a 會發 [æ]，字母 e 會發 [ɛ]，字母 i 會發 [ɪ]，字母 o 會發 [ɑ]，而字母 u 會發 [ʌ]。

　　例如：1. twin 和 inn 字中的 "i" 發 [ɪ] 音，front 字中的 "o" 發 [ɑ] 音，desk 和 pet 字中的 "e" 發 [ɛ] 音。

　　　　　2. single 字的重音在 "sin" 上面，而且這個重音節只有一個母音，所以 "i" 發 [ɪ] 音。

規則二 一個子音加上 "le" 結尾會發 [!] 音。

　　例如：1. single 字中的 "g" 加上 "le" 會發 [g!] 音

　　　　　2. "p" + "le" = [p!]

　　　　　3. "b" + "le" = [b!]

　　　　　4. "t" + "le" = [t!]

　　　　　5. "d" + "le" = [d!]

　　　　　6. "k" + "le" = [k!]

　　　　　7. "f" + "le" = [f!]

規則三 兩個母音 o 會發 [ʊ] 音或 [u] 音；兩個母音 e 會發 [i] 音。

　　例如：book 字中的 "oo" 會發 [ʊ] 音，room 字中的 "oo" 會發 [u] 音
　　　　　greet 字中的 "ee" 會發 [i] 音。

單字表

1. book [bʊk]	(v)預約、預訂 (n)書	例 I have booked a hotel room. This book is mine.
2. double room ['dʌb!'rum]	(n)有一張雙人床的房間	例 There is only one bed in a double room.
3. twin room [twɪn rum]	(n)有兩張床的房間	例 A twin room can hold two to four people.

4. front desk ['frʌnt dɛsk]	(n)櫃檯	例 You should get your key at the front desk.
5. greet [grit]	(v)打招呼	例 I greet my teacher when I see her.
6. pet [pɛt]	(n)寵物	例 John has a pet dog.
7. suite [swit]	(n)套房	例 My suite number is 205.
8. inn [ɪn]	(n)小旅館	例 I stayed in Cambridge Inn for two nights.

Reading

閱讀策略──掃描閱讀法

　　閱讀一篇文章並不一定需要看懂每一個字，而是根據閱讀目地的不同，以不同的閱讀方式來達成目地。例如：下列的飯店訊息需要你用快速掃描的方式，以關鍵字來找到你想要的答案。

　　試著用這個方法勾選下列關於兩家飯店正確的敘述。例如：第一題 "This hotel has twin rooms." 關鍵字是 twin rooms，那麼就掃瞄 twin rooms 這個字在哪裡，即可找到需要的訊息。

A. You and your friend are going to travel to Sun Moon Lake. The Sun Inn and the Lakeside Hotel are two famous hotels by Sun Moon Lake. Read the information about these two hotels below. Check (√) the correct box.

	Sun Inn	Lakeside Hotel
1. This hotel has twin rooms.	☐	☐
2. This hotel has lakeview suites.	☐	☐
3. You do not need to check in.	☐	☐
4. You can't take your dog into the hotel.	☐	☐
5. You will have free breakfast.	☐	☐
6. You can't smoke in your room.	☐	☐
7. You can book online.	☐	☐

The Sun Inn	The Lakeside Hotel
Guest Room	Guest Room

The Sun Inn	The Lakeside Hotel
Room types	**Room types**
➤ Double room	➤ Standard guest room
➤ Twin room	➤ Lakeview suite
➤ Suite	When you arrive at the Lakeside Hotel, there is
All our guest rooms are new and modern.	no need to check in at the front desk. People will
There are hairdryer, tea/coffee, telephone, internet	greet you and take you to your room.
and TV in all rooms.	Free breakfast for all guests.
Check-in time: 3:00 pm.	No smoking in rooms.
Check-out time: 12:00 at noon.	For booking, email to reservations@thelakeside.
Your room will be held until 6:30 pm.	com.tw or call 886-49-2229888
No pets. No cooking.	
You can book online or call 886-49-226655	

Grammar

A. 未來式複習：下列三個句子表達一個未來的動作。這三個句子的文法結構有何不同？
說話者所表達的意思有什麼不同呢？

1. I will spend two nights in the Sun Inn.

    說話者要表達的意思為：＿＿＿＿＿＿＿＿＿＿＿＿＿＿＿＿＿

2. I am going to spend two nights in the Sun Inn.

    說話者要表達的意思為：＿＿＿＿＿＿＿＿＿＿＿＿＿＿＿＿＿

3. I am spending two nights in the Sun Inn.

    說話者要表達的意思為：＿＿＿＿＿＿＿＿＿＿＿＿＿＿＿＿＿

will	表達對未來的預測（prediction）或期望（expectation） 例 I will finish my study in two years.
be going to	表達對未來的意圖（intention） 例 She wants to be a lawyer. She is going to study law.
be -ing	表達對未來的安排（arrangement） 例 The bus is leaving for Taipei at 7:00.

B. 練習下列 **"would prefer"** 句型。你知道 **"would prefer"** 所表達的意思嗎？試著運用這些句型造句。

Would you prefer + Noun?

Would you prefer	the Sun Inn or the Lakeside Hotel? tea or coffee? pen or pencil?

造句　Would you prefer _____?

Would you prefer + Ving/to V ?

Would you prefer	staying/to stay in the Sun Inn or the Lakeside Hotel? drinking/to drink tea or coffee? using/to use a pen or pencil?

造句　Would you prefer _____?

I would (I'd) prefer + Noun.

I would prefer/ I'd prefer	the Sun Inn coffee a pen

造句　I would prefer _____.

I would (I'd) prefer + Ving.

I would prefer/ I'd prefer	staying/to stay in the Lakeside Hotel? drinking/to drink coffee using/to use a pen

造句 I would prefer _____.

Writing

A. Complete the conversations. Use complete sentences.

1. A: Which would you prefer? A standard guest room or a suite.

   B: _____.

2. A: Would you prefer taking a bus or a taxi?

   B: _____. Taking a taxi is too expensive.

3. A: _____.

   B: I've been to Sun Moon Lake before. I'd prefer to take a trip to Kenting.

4. A: Would you prefer _____?

   B: _____.

Speaking

 Track 6

A. Pronunciation. Listen and practice.

1. *I'd* prefer the Sun Inn.

2. *I'd* prefer staying in the Lakeview Hotel.

3. *I'd* prefer to use a pencil.

Note

I would = I'd

B. Which would you prefer? Answer the questions.

Would you prefer ...?	I'd prefer ...
1. the Sun Inn or the Lakeside Hotel	
2. tea or coffee	
3. using a pen or a pencil	
4. eating rice or noodles	
5. buying a car or taking a bus	
6. _____	

C. Practice asking your classmates these questions. Write their names and answers in the boxes.

Would you prefer ...?	Name	Answer
1. the Sun Inn or the Lakeside Hotel		
2. tea or coffee		
3. using a pen or a pencil		
4. eating rice or noodles		
5. buying a car or taking a bus		
6. _____		

D. Report your survey results. You may use the following sentence patterns.

20% of my interviewees would prefer ...

50% of my interviewees would prefer ...

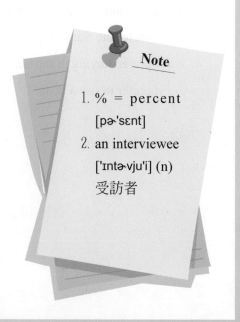

Note

1. % = percent
   [pɚ'sɛnt]
2. an interviewee
   ['ɪntɚˌvju'i] (n)
   受訪者

Listening

🎵 Track 7

A. Hotel room booking. Listen to people calling to book hotel rooms. Would they prefer the Sun Inn or the Lakeside Hotel? Match the names with the correct hotel. The first one has been done for you.

1. Lydia   Sun Inn

2. Hank

3. Alan   Lakeside Hotel

4. Julie

💡 **聽力策略——練習聽特定的訊息**

　　當我們在聽英語對話或訊息時，我們並不需要聽懂每一個英文字才算聽懂。我們只要抓住訊息的重點或聽懂我們想要知道的訊息就是成功的聽力理解！在接下來 B 部份的聽力練習裡，你必須要聽到的是 Room types，所以 room 還有在前面的單元裡學到的 double room, twin room, suite, king guest room 等就成了關鍵字。至於 check-in 和 check-out time 所需要聽懂的就是——數字。你還記得 1 到 12 的英文要怎麼說嗎？現在就注意聽 room types 和數字吧！

🎵 Track 8

B. Listen again. Complete the chart.

	Room type	**Check-in time**	**Check-out time**
1. Lydia	*standard guest room*		
2. Hank			
3. Alan			
4. Julie			

ESP

Working as a hotel receptionist：A hotel receptionist has to deal with restaurant and hotel bookings, checking guests in and out, applying charges to bills, and dealing with payments.

A. The following questions are commonly asked by hotel receptionists:

1. How may I help you?
2. When was the reservation for?
3. Is the booking for one night or two?
4. What is your first name?
5. May I have your surname?
6. Could you spell your surname for me, please?
7. Would you mind repeating that, please?
8. How would you like to pay?
9. Is there anything else?

中文	英文
王小明	Shiao-ming, Wang
林美玲	Mei-ling, Lin

Shiao-ming 是「名」，英文為 first name 或者是 given name；Wang 是「姓」，英文為 last name 或 surname 又或是 family name。

寫下你的 first name 以及 last name：

First name: _____

Last name: _____

B. Work in pairs. Choose one situation. Use the questions in Exercise A to make up a conversation.

Situation 1: You are a hotel receptionist. Your partner calls for making a reservation. Ask him/her for the date of traveling and the room type.

Situation 2: You are a receptionist. Your partner calls to confirm a reservation. Ask your partner his/her name. Check his/her reservation.

Situation 3: You are a hotel receptionist. Your partner lost his/her room key. He/she comes to the front desk to tell you about it. Help him/her solve this problem.

Unit **3**

Food

Warm Up

A. Match the food with the name above.

   a. doughnut

   b. pudding

   c. tofu

   d. wonton

☐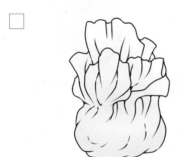

☐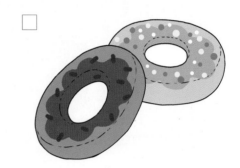

☐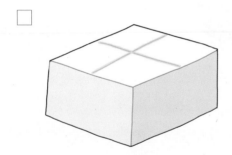

☐

B. What is special about those names?

Vocabulary

💡單字策略——譯音相近法

　　試著唸唸看下列這些單字，你是否能夠聯想到它們的意思呢？

     1. doughnut ['do'nʌt] → 多拿滋 → 油炸圈餅；甜甜圈

     2. pudding ['pʊdɪŋ] → 布丁

     3. tofu ['tofu] → 豆腐

     4. wonton ['wʌntʌn] → 餛飩

單字表

1. doughnut ['do'nʌt]	(n)油炸圈餅；甜甜圈	例 Do you want to try my home-made doughnut?
2. pudding ['pʊdɪŋ]	(n)布丁	例 Children like to eat puddings for dessert.
3. tofu ['tofu]	(n)豆腐	例 Tofu is a kind of soft white food made from soy milk.
4. appetizer ['æpə'taɪzɚ]	(n)開胃的食物，開胃小吃	例 What appetizer do you want to try before dinner?
5. main dish [men dɪʃ]	(n)主菜	例 How many kinds of main dish does this restaurant provide?
6. dessert [dɪ'zɝt]	(n)甜點心；餐後甜點	例 Desserts are usually served after main dishes.
7. beverage ['bɛvərɪdʒ]	(n)飲料	例 Cokes and sodas are beverages.
8. cold dish [kold dɪʃ]	(n)冷盤	例 We usually have some cold dishes before our main dish.
9. shake [ʃek]	(n)奶昔，冰淇淋雪泡	例 That restaurant is famous for their milk shake.
10. cucumber ['kjukʌmbɚ]	(n)黃瓜，胡瓜	例 Have you ever tried cucumber juice?
11. eggplant ['ɛg'plænt]	(n)茄子	例 The skin of an eggplant is usually purple.

12. stir-fried [stɝ fraɪd]	(adj)炒的	例 How do you like your vegetables to be done? Steamed or stir-fried?
13. dumpling ['dʌmplɪŋ]	(n)水餃	例 Many Chinese families eat dumplings on Chinese New Year Eve.
14. wonton ['wʌntʌn]	(n)餛飩	例 Wonton noodle soup is John's favorite Chinese food.
15. hot and sour [hɑt ænd saʊr]	(n)酸辣	例 People often have hot and sour soup after eating dumplings.
16. water spinach ['wɔtɚ 'spɪnɪdʒ]	(n)空心菜	例 Stir-fried water spinach is a popular dish in Taiwan.

💡單字策略──單字分類幫助記憶

　　背單字的時候可以先想出單字的屬性，然候將同樣屬性的單字歸類在一起，例如：corn soup, chicken soup 都屬於 soup 湯類。

請依照下列食物找出屬於它們的屬性，並將屬性填入空格中

chocolate shake	pudding	cheeseburger	hot dog
doughnut	green salad	potato skin	dried tofu
cucumber salad	stir-fried chicken noodle	dumpling	green tea
wonton soup	black tea	hot and sour soup	coke

Appetizer/Cold Dish	Main Dish	Soup	Dessert	Beverage

Reading

A. Read the following two advertisements. Which restaurant would you like to try?

Yummy's Special Offer
American Food Available

Appetizer:

Green salad/Potato skins

Main Dish:

Cheeseburger/Hot dog

Dessert:

Doughnut/Pudding

Beverage:

Chocolate shake/Coke

NT$200 Per Person

10% Service Charge

Special Offer Time: Mon-Fri 11 am-5 pm

No. 1, Big Wind Rd.,

Taichung, Taiwan

(04) 23585892

www.yummy.com.tw

Stop by and experience us!

Dali's All-You-Can-Eat
Chinese Food Available

Cold dish:

Dried tofu/cucumber salad

Stir-fried Vegetables:

Water spinach/Eggplants

Main Dish:

Stir-fried chicken noodles/ Dumplings

Soup:

Wonton soup/Hot and sour soup

Beverage:

Green tea/ Black tea

NT$300 Per Person No Service Charge

Offer Available: Mon-Fri 11 am-10 pm

No. 75, Deep Water Rd.,

Taichung, Taiwan

(04) 23532598

www.dali.com.tw

Welcome to join us!

如何快速地找到你要的資訊呢？

當你在看菜單的時候，你可以快速地掃描菜單上面的線索字，例如：appetizer 表示前菜類，main dish 表示主菜類，如果你要找喝的東西，就必須找到線索字 beverage 表示飲料；如果要找價格就必須快速掃描金錢符號及數字部份。

B. Read the advertisements and answer the following questions.

_____ 1. If you want to eat hamburgers, which restaurant should you go to?

　　　(A) Yummy　　　(B) Dali

_____ 2. If you want to find tea, which part should you read?

　　　(A) Appetizer　　　(B) Dessert　　　(C) Beverage　　　(D) Cold dish

_____ 3. If you want more detail about Dali's All-You-Can-Eat, what should you do?

　　　(A) Visit **www.yummy.com.tw**　　　(B) Visit **www.dali.com.tw**

　　　(C) Go to Big Wind Road　　　(D) Call at (04) 23585892

C. Read the advertisements again and answer the following questions.

1. Which restaurant is cheaper?

　_____ is cheaper than _____

2. How much will Grace spend if she tries Yummy's Special Offer?

　She needs to spend _____ dollars in total.

Grammar

Comparisons with Adjectives（形容詞的比較級）：比較人物、事情、地點、東西及動作。
形容詞比較級的形式如下：
形容詞字尾加上 *-er, -r, -ier*

Adjectives	Comparative
cheap	cheaper
rich	richer
fresh	fresher
tasty	tastier
yummy	yummier
healthy	healthier

形容詞前面加上 "*more*"

Adjectives	Comparative
delicious	more delicious
comfortable	more comfortable
popular	more popular
reasonable	more reasonable

不規則的形容詞比較級

Adjectives	Comparative
good	better
bad	worse

形容詞比較兩種東西時，使用的方法可分下列兩種：

Sentence Pattern A				
A	Be V	Adj-er/more Adj	than	B
Yummy's price	is	cheaper	than	Dali's
Dali's food	is	more delicious	than	Yummy's

Sentence Pattern B				
A	Be V	the	Adj-er/more Adj	of the two
Yummy's price	is	the	cheaper	of the two
Dali's food	is	the	more delicious	of the two

Writing

A. The Food Commentary Website wants your comments on Yummy's and Dali's Restaurants. Write five sentences to compare these two restaurants on the weblog.

1. I think _____ is _____ than _____ .

2. In my mind, _____ is _____ than _____ .

3. I believe the food of _____ is _____ than that of _____ .

4. In my opinion, the price of _____ is _____ than that of _____ .

5. All in all, _____ is the _____ of the two.

Speaking

A. Look at the advertisements for Yummy's and Dali's Restaurants again. Which restaurant do you want to try? Use the expressions shown below.

Interviewer	Interviewee
🗣Which restaurant do you want to try?	🗣I'd like ... 🗣I prefer ... to ... 🗣I would like to try ...
🗣Why do you want to try it?	🗣In my opinion, ... is [cheaper, richer, yummier, tastier, better, nicer, more mouth-watering, more delicious, more comfortable, more popular] than... 🗣I think the ... in ... is more reasonable, fresher, more flavorful, healthier] than that in ...

B. Use the expressions introduced above to interview five classmates. Which restaurant would most classmates like? Why?Complete the following interview chart.

	Names of the classmates	Restaurants	Reasons
1			
2			
3			
4			
5			

Listening

💡聽力策略──注意結尾子音與連音

　　當你在唸句子的時候，遇到子音結尾的字加上母音開頭的字，唸快一點的時候會自然形成連音現象。

A. Let's practice the following sounds

1. come on [kʌmɑn]

2. have a seat [hævə]

🎵 Track 10

B. Practice the sentences below

1. I hope you like it.

2. Let's find a burger place.

3. That's a good idea.

4. I want to have a pudding.

5. That's a total of NT $400.

🎵 Track 11

C. Listen to the dialogue and check the dishes they are talking about.

Dali's All-You-Can-Eat Menu

Cold Dish

☐ Dried tofu   ☐ Cucumber salad

Stir-fried Vegetable

☐ Water spinach   ☐ Eggplants

Main Dish

☐ Stir-fried chicken noodles ☐ Dumplings

💡 聽力策略──預測技巧

　　聽重要訊息的時候可以運用所聽到的線索字來預測說話者接下來要說的內容。例如：聽到 main dish 時可以知道說話者將要說出所點的主菜，此時就把聽力的重點放在主菜部分。

🎵 Track 12

D. Listen to the dialogue again and choose the correct answer.

_____ 1. What kind of food does the restaurant serve?

　　(A) Chinese food　　　　　　(B) American food

_____ 2. What kind of food does Jean like?

    (A) Chinese food   (B) American food

_____ 3. Why do they want to find a burger place next time?

    (A) The restaurant is too expensive for them to afford.

    (B) The food is not delicious for John and Jean.

    (C) The service is terrible and the food is bad.

    (D) The restaurant is not the type that Jean likes.

ESP

Working as a waiter/waitress: A waiter or waitress has to deal with taking orders for customers.

A. Practice the expressions that are commonly used when taking orders:

Situations	What waiters/waitress say	What customers say
Taking orders	🗣 May I help you, sir / madam? 🗣 May I take your order? 🗣 What would you like to order?	🗣 I'd like ... 🗣 I'll have... 🗣 May I try some of your ...? 🗣 Please give me... 🗣 May I have...?
Asking for further information	🗣 Anything else? 🗣 Do you want...? 🗣 Would you like...?	🗣 May I have some more..., please? 🗣 Can you give me some more..., please? 🗣 I would like to have some more..., please?
Asking if customers would like to take the meal out	🗣 For here or to go? 🗣 Will you be eating here?	🗣 I'd like it to go. 🗣 To go, please. 🗣 For here.

B. Find a partner to have a role play. One acts as a waiter/waitress, the other as a customer. You may use the following menus to order food or take orders.

For the customer	For the waiter/waitress
Dali's All-You-Can-Eat	**Dali's All-You-Can-Eat**
Cold dish	Cold dish
☐ Dried tofu	☐ Dried tofu
☐ Cucumber salad	☐ Cucumber salad
Stir-fried Vegetables	Stir-fried Vegetables
☐ Water spinach	☐ Water spinach
☐ Eggplants	☐ Eggplants
Main Dish	Main Dish
☐ Stir-fried chicken noodle	☐ Stir-fried chicken noodle
☐ Dumplings	☐ Dumplings
Soup	Soup
☐ Wonton soup	☐ Wonton soup
☐ Hot and sour soup	☐ Hot and sour soup
Beverage	Beverage
☐ Green tea	☐ Green tea
☐ Black tea	☐ Black tea

C. Switch your role with your partner.

Unit **4**

Travel & Flight

Warm up

A. Match the word with its correct meaning.

_____	1. an itinerary	a. 起程、出發
_____	2. a flight	b. 旅行的行程
_____	3. to depart	c. 經濟艙
_____	4. to arrive at	d. 到達、抵達
_____	5. a passenger	e. 班機
_____	6. an aircraft	f. 航廈
_____	7. a cabin	g. 飛機、航空器
_____	8. the economy class	h. 乘客、旅客
_____	9. terminal	i. 座艙
_____	10. to board	j. 上船、登機

Vocabulary

💡單字策略──故事串連法

1. 想要把上述的單字記起來並不難，你可以用故事把這些字串聯起來，這樣一來單字記憶就變得容易多了！

例如：Amy 要搭機到美國 → 她來到機場的 **Terminal 1** → 她是一個 **passenger** → 她拿出她的**itinerary** 查看搭機的時間 → 在 8:15 AM 的時候，她的 **flight** 即將 **depart** 並將於當地時間下午兩點 **arrive at** 美國 → 在等候時，她隔著玻璃窗看見幾架 **aircrafts** → 終於要 **board** 了！她進入了 **cabin** → 找到她在 **economy class** 的位子。

2.現在拿一張紙把上面的故事和單字解釋遮起來，用下列的單字再把故事說一次。試
  試看！你還記得這個故事和這些單字的意思嗎？

an itinerary	a flight	to depart		to arrive	a passenger
an aircraft	a cabin	the economy class	terminal	to board

單字表

1. itinerary [aɪ'tɪnə'rɛrɪ]	(n)旅程；路線	例 John read the itinerary to check his flight number.
2. flight [flaɪt]	(n)班次；班機；飛機的航程	例 Please remain seated during the flight.
3. depart [dɪ'pɑrt]	(v)起程、出發	例 We will depart from Kaohsiung.
4. arrive [ə'raɪv]	(v)到達	例 She arrived at the airport at 4:30 pm.
5. passenger ['pæsṇdʒɚ]	(n)乘客、旅客	例 There are three passengers in the car.
6. aircraft ['ɛr,kræft]	(n)航空器；飛機	例 This aircraft can carry more than 300 passengers.
7. cabin ['kæbɪn]	(n)客艙	例 Cecilia asked the cabin crew where her seat was.
8. economy class [ɪ'kɑnəmɪ klæs]	(n)經濟艙位	例 Seats are smaller in the economy class cabin.

9. terminal ['tɜ·mənl]	(n)航空站	例 Our flight will be arriving at Terminal 3 of the airport.		
10. board [bord]	(v)上（船、車、飛機等）	例 The passengers are ready to board the plane.		

Reading

A. Amy is going to travel to America for Christmas. This is her flight itinerary. Which city is Amy going to?

Itinerary

Passenger: Chen/Amy

Date		City/ Terminal	Time	Flight/ Cabin	Aircraft Type/ Travel Time/ Services
12/20/2012	**Departing**	Taipei Terminal 1	8:34	U342 Economy	Boeing 737 Operated by US Air
	Arriving	Tokyo Terminal 1	12:47		3 hr 13 min N/A
12/20/2012	**Departing**	Tokyo Terminal 2	13:05	U745 Economy	Boeing 747 Operated by US Air
	Arriving	New York Terminal 3	15:52		14 hr 13 min 2 meals
1/8/2013	**Departing**	New York Terminal 2	11:15	U208 Economy	Boeing 747 Operated by US Air
	Arriving	Tokyo Terminal 1	13:50		14 hr 35 min 2 meals
1/9/2013	**Departing**	Tokyo Terminal 1	17:23	U512 Economy	Airbus 300 Operated by
	Arriving	Taipei Terminal 2	19:25		Formosa Airway 3 hr 02 min 1 meal

閱讀策略——快速理解圖表內容

　　看到一個表格的時候應該先看橫軸和縱軸，也就是最上列和最左欄。現在趕快看一下這個電子機票的最上列和最左欄，它們告訴你什麼訊息呢？是不是根據最上列和最左欄你要知道的訊息，找到它們的交叉點就是了。

　　例如：如果你想知道 Amy 在 12 月 20 日的班機什麼時候起飛，你就應該從最左欄的 12/20/2012 departing 和最上欄的 time 著手，並找出它們的交叉點，就是答案了！現在就試著用這個方法回答下列的問題。

B. Read again. Answer the following questions.

1. What time will Amy's flight depart from Tokyo? _____
2. Which terminal will Amy arrive at in New York? _____
3. When will Amy leave America? _____
4. What type of aircraft will Amy take from New York to Tokyo? _____
5. Which is Amy's cabin? The first class, business class or economy class? _____
6. Will Amy have a meal on Flight U342? _____
7. How long does it take for Amy to fly from New York to Tokyo? _____

Listening

Track 13

A. Listen to the announcement. Where can you hear this announcement? Circle the correct place.

In a bus station　　On an aircraft　　In an airport　　On a train

聽力策略——聽關鍵字

　　聽懂英語並不需要聽懂每一個字，而是聽懂關鍵字，再根據關鍵字推測可能的情境來幫助理解。

　　例如：A 部份聽力的關鍵字為 passenger, flight 及 board，而聽到 to begin boarding 表示還沒有在飛機上，由此可推斷出這個廣播發生在機場裡，而不是公車站或火車上，因為公車站或火車上的廣播不會有 flight 出現。

　　現在就用這個方法完成下面的練習吧！

B. Listen to four announcements. Write down the key words that you hear. Circle the correct place where you can hear these announcements.

1. In a bus station   In a department store   In an airport   On a train

   Key words: _____

2. In a bus station   In a department store   On an aircraft   On a train

   Key words: _____

3. In a bus station   In a department store   In an airport   On a train

   Key words: _____

4. In a bus station   In a department store   On an aircraft   On a train

   Key words: _____

Writing

A. During the flight, Amy is asked to fill in the I-94 Arrival/Departure Record because she is not a U.S. citizen. Use the information given below to help Amy fill up the form.

Name (Surname, Given name)	Passport No.
Chen, Amy	223411003
Nationality	**Personal ID No**
REPUBLIC OF CHINA	Z334998809
Sex: F	**Date of birth:**
Date of issue	20 March 1990
5 May 2008	
Date of expiry	
5 May 2018	

DEPARTMENT OF HOMELAND SECURITY
U.S. Customs and Border Protection

Welcome to the United States
I-94 Arrival/Departure Record
Instructions

This form must be completed by all persons except U.S. Citizens, returning resident aliens, aliens with immigrant visas, and Canadian Citizens visiting or in transit.

Type of print legibly with pen in ALL CAPITAL LETTERS. Use English. Do not write on the back of this form.

This form is in two parts. Please complete both the Arrival Record (Item 1 through 17) and the Departure Record (Item 18 through 21.)

When all items are completed present this form to the CBP Officer.

Item 9 – If you are entering the United States by land, enter LAND in this space. If you are entering the United States by ship, enter SEA in this space.

Arrival Record
Admission Number
491755175 21

1. Family Name
   C H E N

2. First (Given) Name   3. Birth Date (DD/MM/YY)

4. Country of Citizenship   5. Sex (Male or Female)

6. Passport Issue Date (DD/MM/YY)   7. Passport Expiration Date (DD/MM/YY)

8. Passport Number   9. Airline and Flight Number

10. Country Where You Live   11. Country Where You Boarded

12. City Where Visa Was Issued   13. Date Issued (DD/MM/YY)
   1 4 0 7 2 0 1 2

14. Address While in the United States (Number and Street)

15. City and State

16. Telephone Number in the U.S. Where You can be Reached

17. Email Address

DEPARTMENT OF HOMELAND SECURITY
U.S. Customs and Border Protection
Departure Record
Admission Number
491755175 21

18. Family Name

19. First (Given) Name   20. Birth Date (DD/MM/YY)

21. Country of Citizenship

Grammar

A. 閱讀下列句子。直接問句與間接問句有何不同？你能找出它們的文法規則嗎？

直接問句（**Direct Questions**）

Is Broadway around here?
Is Central Park near Times Square?
Where is the Statue of Liberty?
How far is Yankee Stadium?
What is special on Wall Street?

間接問句（**Indirect Questions**）

Can you tell me Could you tell me Do you know	if Broadway is around here? whether Central Park is near Times Square?
	where the Statue of Liberty is? how far Yankee Stadium is?
	What is special on Wall Street?

B. 將下列句子改為間接問句。

1. Is Broadway around here?

   Can you tell me _____?

2. Is Central Park near Times Square?

   Could you tell me _____?

3. Where is the Statue of Liberty?

   Do you know _____?

4. How far is Yankee Stadium?

   Do you know _____?

5. What is special on Wall Street?

   Can you tell me _____?

Speaking

A. Look at the map of New York City. Work in pairs.

Student A: You are Amy. You are going to the Yankee Stadium, Wall Street and Central Park. Ask your partner the questions you have just learned in the grammar section.

Student B: Answer Student A's questions.

B. Change roles.

Student A: Answer Student B's questions.

Student B: You are Amy. You are going to see the Statue of Liberty, Brooklyn Bridge and to watch a show in Broadway. Ask the questions you have just learned in the grammar section.

You may use these sentences to answer questions:

🗣 It is about 2 kilometers from here.

🗣 It is on Ellis Island.

🗣 There are many nice shops and restaurants.

🗣 No, it is far away from Times Square.

🗣 Yes, it's just one block away.

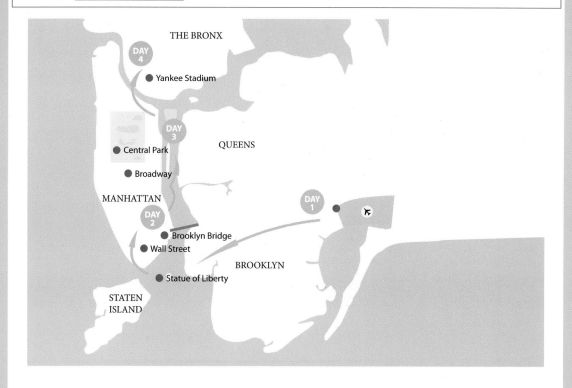

ESP

A. A tourist guide leads a group of travelers to visit a place, a city or a country. A tourist guide has to introduce and explain a place where their group goes to.

For example:

Now we're heading to Lukang. Lukang was the second largest town in Taiwan during the 18th century. The town was the gateway to central Taiwan. There are many temples and historical places in Lukang. The Lung-Shan temple, Tien-Hou Temple, and Wen-Kai Academy are the most famous. The Lung-Shan temple was built in 1786. It was called the Taiwan Palace. The Tien-Hou Temple was built in 1683. It is a place to worship Mazu. Wen-Kai Academy is the place where old Lukang people studied. By the way, don't forget to try some seafood, fengyan cake, and meat buns when you visit Lukang.

B. Imagine a group of foreigners are planning to take a day trip to your hometown. How would you introduce your hometown to them? Talk about...

1. *History/background*
2. *Tourist attractions*
3. *Food*
4. *Crafts*
5. *Others*

Unit **5**

Warm Up

　　以下這三個單字，是在衣服標籤上面常常看到的，試著念出這些單字，你可以聯想到它們的意思嗎？先唸出下面的單字，再依照單字的發音連到相對應的中文意思。

1. Cashmere ['kæʃmɪr]　　　　a. 尼龍；尼龍襪

2. silk [sɪlk]　　　　　　　　b. 喀什米爾羊毛織品；羊絨

3. nylon ['naɪlɑn]　　　　　　c. 蠶絲，絲；絲織物（品），綢布

Vocabulary

單字表

1. top [tɑp]	(n)上衣	例 The top of a nurse's uniform is usually white.
2. blouse [blauz]	(n)（婦女，兒童等的）短上衣，短衫	例 The blouse is a kind of top that women wear.
3. overcoat ['ovɚ'kot]	(n)外套，大衣	例 You will need an overcoat when it is cold.
4. shorts [ʃɔrts]	(n)短褲	例 We usually wear shorts at home.
5. trousers ['trauzɚz]	(n)褲子；長褲	例 Recently many women like to wear trousers.
6. slacks [slæks]	(n)寬鬆的長褲；便褲	例 Many people wear slacks at home.
7. leggings ['lɛgɪŋs]	(n)綁腿褲（緊身褲）	例 Leggings are a kind of fitted pants covering the legs.
8. Cashmere ['kæʃmɪr]	(n)喀什米爾羊毛織品	例 This coat is made up of 100% Cashmere.
9. silk [sɪlk]	(n)蠶絲，絲；絲織物（品），綢布	例 Some places in China are famous for producing fine silk.
10. cotton ['kɑtn̩]	(n)棉，棉花，棉屬植物	例 Cotton can be used to make comfortable clothing.
11. polyester ['pɑlɪ'ɛstɚ]	(n)聚酯；人造纖維	例 Clothing made of polyester is easier to clean.

12. rayon ['reɑn]	(n)嫘縈；人造絲，人造纖維	例 Rayon is very popular for making blouses or dresses.
13. wool [wʊl]	(n)羊毛	例 Wool is taken from the hair of the animals like sheep, goats, or rabbits.
14. spandex ['spæn'dɛks]	(n)作腰帶、泳衣用的彈性人造纖維	例 Spandex fiber （纖維） is used for making swimsuits, ski pants, and leggings.
15. nylon ['naɪlɑn]	(n)尼龍	例 People like to use nylon to make ropes because it is endurable.
16. chlorine ['klorɪn]	(n)氯	例 Chlorine is often used in swimming pools to keep water clean.
17. tumble dry ['tʌmbl̩ draɪ]	(v)烘乾	例 After we tumble dry wool clothing, it usually becomes smaller.
18. soak [sok]	(v)浸泡	例 The blouse cannot be soaked in warm water.
19. bleach [blitʃ]	(v)漂白	例 I want to bleach this white shirt because it is very dirty.

💡單字技巧──單字分類法

　　背單字的時候可以先想出單字的屬性，然後將同樣屬性的單字歸類在一起，例如：jeans, shorts, trousers 都屬於 pants 褲子類。

請將下列單字依照衣服的屬性填入所屬的類別

T-shirt	jeans	blouse	shorts	shirt
trousers	jacket	slacks	overcoat	leggings

上衣類	褲子類

Reading

💡閱讀策略──圖片猜測技巧

　　如何利用圖片猜測文字可能的意思呢？

　　當你看到衣服上面的標籤，你可以先看標籤上面的圖形，例如由圖型上面來猜測衣服保養的方式，例如熨斗的圖形代表燙熨的方式。

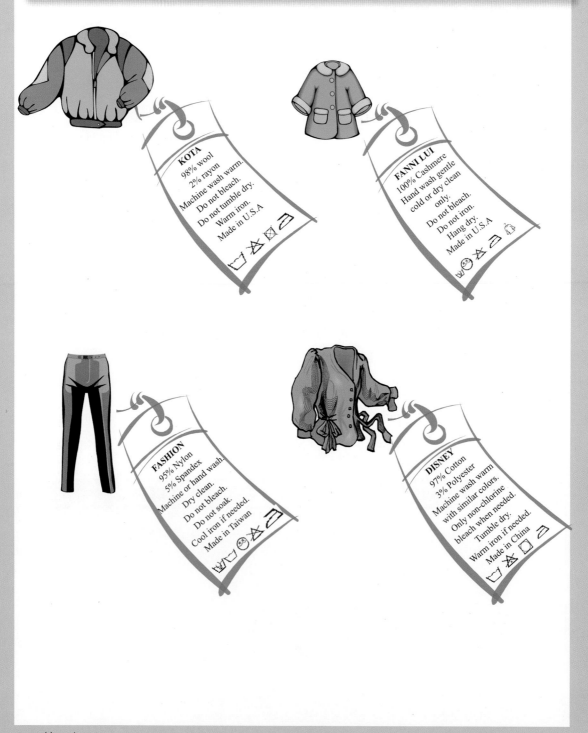

KOTA
98% wool
2% rayon
Machine wash warm.
Do not bleach.
Do not tumble dry.
Warm iron.
Made in U.S.A

FANNI LUI
100% Cashmere
Hand wash gentle
cold or dry clean
only.
Do not bleach.
Do not iron.
Hang dry.
Made in U.S.A

FASHION
95% Nylon
5% Spandex
Machine or hand wash.
Dry clean.
Do not bleach.
Do not soak.
Cool iron if needed.
Made in Taiwan

DISNEY
97% Cotton
3% Polyester
Machine wash warm
with similar colors.
Only non-chlorine
bleach when needed.
Tumble dry.
Warm iron if needed.
Made in China

A. Read the labels, then check ☑ or cross ☒ the steps according to the labels.

Jacket	Overcoat	Leggings	Blouse
☐ ironed	☐ ironed	☐ ironed	☐ ironed
☐ washed by machines	☐ washed by machines	☐ washed by machines	☐ washed by machines
☐ bleached	☐ bleached	☐ bleached	☐ bleached
☐ tumble dried	☐ tumble dried	☐ soaked	☐ tumble dried
Made in _____	Made in _____	Made in _____	Made in _____

Grammar

Passive Voice（被動語態）：被動語態中，主動語態動詞的受詞成為被動語態動詞的主詞，主動語態動詞的主詞在被動語態中接在 by 之後。

	主動語態	被動語態
現在式	Mary irons the blouse. Jane washes the leggings.	The blouses are ironed by Mary. The leggings are washed by Jane.
過去式	Mary washed the trousers. John bleached the shirt.	The trousers were washed by Mary. The shirt was bleached by John.
未來式	Mary will soak the overcoat. Lucy will tumble dry the skirt.	The overcoat will be soaked by Mary. The skirt will be tumble dried by Lucy.

A. 你能夠找出被動語態的公式嗎？

現在簡單被動式→ S + _____ + _____ + _____ + O

過去簡單被動式→ S + _____ + _____ + _____ + O

未來簡單被動式→ S + _____ + _____ + _____ +

_____ + O

被動語態最常用在執行動作者不明確，或是沒有必要知道執行動作者的時候，在這種情況下則by通常可以省略。

例如：The shorts cannot be bleached.

例如：The slacks cannot be tumble dried.

Writing

You want to bring your clothes to the laundry. Take a look at the labels of the clothes you want to wash and complete the form below. Write at least two special instructions by using the passive voice "... cannot be..."

Laundry

Name:	Date:
Please check	
☐ Regular service (within 1 day)	☐ Express service (within 4 hours)
☐ Return clothes folded	☐ Return clothes on hangers
Special Instructions:	
Signature:	

Speaking

 金額的唸法

　　表達金額的時候，需注意代表金額單位的語詞：百為 hundred，千為 thousand，非整數金額時，可在最後兩位數字前加上 and，最後再加上貨幣名稱 [USD = US dollar; NT = NT dollar（新台幣）; JPY = Japanese Yen（日圓）; THB = Thai Baht（泰銖）]。例如：NT $ 420 唸成 "four hundred and twenty NT dollars."

A. Orally read the following prices

1. USD　　$ 125
2. NTD　　$ 248
3. JPY　　$ 3,524
4. THB　　$ 8,946

B. Take a look at the advertisement of Queen Department Store. You and your partner would like to buy a birthday present for your best friend. You have about $1,000 NT dollars. Which clothes will you buy? You may use the following sentence patterns.

Queen Department Store

Sale! Today Only! 50% Off All Items

Tops	prices		50% off	Pants	prices		50% off
T-shirt	NT $ 50	→	NT$ 25	jeans	NT $ 250	→	NT$ 125
blouse	NT $ 130	→	NT$ 65	shorts	NT $ 240	→	NT$ 120
shirt	NT $ 150	→	NT$ 75	trousers	NT $ 350	→	NT$ 175
jacket	NT $ 1,000	→	NT$500	slacks	NT $ 420	→	NT$ 210
overcoat	NT $2,000	→	NT$ 1,000	leggings	NT $ 120	→	NT$ 60

Sizes: Small, Medium, Large, and Extra Large!!

Sentence patterns you can use:

🗣 How about buying ...?	🗣 I think ... is cheap. It's ....
🗣 What do you think if we buy ...?	🗣 In my opinion, the price of ... is reasonable. It's...
🗣 What's your opinion?	🗣 ... only costs $ ... NT dollars.
🗣 Why don't you buy ...?	🗣 We may spend only ... for ....
	🗣 ... is/are in our budget with a total of $ ...NT dollars.

Listening

 發音技巧

練習下列數字的發音

十幾的唸法 13, 14, 15, 16, 17, 18, 19

thirteen	fourteen	fifteen	sixteen
['θɝ'tin]	['for'tin]	['fɪf'tin]	['sɪks'tin]

seventeen	eighteen	nineteen
[ˌsɛvən'tin]	['e'tin]	[naɪn'tin]

幾十的唸法 30, 40, 50, 60, 70, 80, 90

thirty	forty	fifty	sixty	seventy	eighty	ninety
['θɝtɪ]	['fɔrtɪ]	['fɪftɪ]	['sɪkstɪ]	['sɛvəntɪ]	['etɪ]	['naɪntɪ]

聽到數字的時候可以把聽到的數字，先轉化成阿拉伯數字，之後把阿拉伯數字寫下來，這樣可以將所聽到的訊息快速地變成可以理解的數字，並且加深對數字的印象。

Track 15

A. Listen to the statements and take notes on the prices. The first one has been done for you.

1. THB $ 1,000
2. ____ $_____
3. ____ $_____
4. ____ $_____
5. ____ $_____

6. ____ $_____
7. ____ $_____
8. ____ $_____
9. ____ $_____
10. ____ $_____

11. ____ $_____
12. ____ $_____
13. ____ $_____
14. ____ $_____
15. ____ $_____

Track 16

B. Listen to the dialogue and choose the correct answer.

_____ 1. What is the discount for the gray blouse?

(A) 13% off   (B) 30% off

(C) 70% off   (D) 3% off

_____ 2. How much does the gray blouse cost?

(A) THB $ 990   (B) THB $ 919

(C) THB $ 900   (D) THB $ 909

_____ 3. How much does the light gray blouse cost?

(A) THB $ 559   (B) THB $ 519

(C) THB $ 509   (D) THB $ 599

_____ 4. Which of the following statements best describes the light gray blouse?

(A) It is machine washed   (B) It is hand washed

(C) It can be bleached   (D) It can be tumble dried

ESP

Working as a clerk in a department store.

A clerk has to deal with customer service.

A. Practice the expressions that are commonly used when serving customers:

Clerk	Customer
🗣 May I help you? 🗣 How may I help you?	🗣 Thank you. I'm just looking. 🗣 I'd like … . 🗣 I would like to see some … . 🗣 I am looking for … . 🗣 I need something to go with my … .
🗣 Our … is/are in this section. 🗣 Our … is/are on sale now. 🗣 What's your size?	🗣 I take small/medium/large size. 🗣 May I try this on?
🗣 Our fitting room is over there. 🗣 Are you doing OK? 🗣 How did it fit you? 🗣 How about this one? 🗣 How do they fit?	🗣 This is too … for me. 🗣 Do you have smaller/bigger size? 🗣 It fits perfectly. 🗣 This style doesn't suit me.
🗣 Cash or charge? 🗣 I'm sorry. Sale items cannot be discounted.	🗣 Cash/charge, please. 🗣 Can you give me a discount?

B. Work in pairs. Use the expressions above to make a conversation.

<u>**Situation 1**</u>: You are a clerk. Your customer wants to find a gold blouse and black trousers.

<u>**Situation 2**</u>: You are a customer. You want to buy a T-shirt which is made up of 100% cotton and is on sale.

Unit **6**

Health

Warm Up

A. Do you know the symptoms of some sicknesses? Write down the sicknesses based on the (symptoms) shown in the picture. （可複選）

（Sicknesses: common cold, flu, asthma）

Symptom	Symptom
Possible sickness(es)	Possible sickness(es)
Symptom	**Symptom**
Possible sickness(es)	Possible sickness(es)
Symptom	**Symptom**
Possible sickness(es)	Possible sickness(es)

B. Have you ever had the symptoms mentioned above? What do you usually do when you have these symptoms?

Vocabulary

💡單字策略──拆字法

　　試著將下面的單字拆開，你就可以從部份的單字猜出這個單字的意思。

1. runny nose = runny 水分過多的 + nose 鼻子 → 流鼻水

2. stuffy nose = stuffy 塞住的 + nose 鼻子 → 鼻塞

3. antibiotic = anti 反對 + biotic 生物的 → 抗生素

4. antiviral drug = anti 反對 + viral 病毒的 + drug 藥品 → 抗病毒藥物

5. breathlessness = breath 呼吸 + less 否定 + -ness 表名詞 → 呼吸急促

6. chest tightness = chest 胸部 + tight 緊的 + -ness 表名詞 → 胸悶

單字表

1. runny nose ['rʌnɪ noz]	(n)流鼻水	例 What causes a runny nose during a cold?
2. symptom ['sɪmptəm]	(n)徵兆	例 A runny nose is one of the symptoms of the common cold.
3. stuffy nose ['stʌfɪ noz]	(n)鼻塞	例 I got a stuffy nose so it's hard for me to take a breath.
4. sore throat [sor θrot]	(n)喉嚨痛	例 The weather was turning cold; my son got a sore throat last night.
5. sneeze [sniz]	(n)打噴嚏	例 My friend caught a cold and sneezed a lot.
6. fever ['fivɚ]	(n)發燒	例 The sick old man had a fever three days ago, but now he is fine.
7. diarrhea ['daɪə'riə]	(n)腹瀉	例 I have had diarrhea since last night.
8. vomit ['vɑmɪt]	(n)嘔吐	例 The food was so terrible that it made me vomit.
9. breathlessness ['brɛθlɪsnɪs]	(n)呼吸急促	例 The drug will cause the patient to have symptoms of breathlessness.

10. chest tightness [tʃɛst 'taɪtnɪs]	(n)胸悶	例 Chest tightness is one of the symptoms of asthma.
11. antibiotic ['æntɪbaɪ'ɑtɪk]	(n)抗生素	例 Take some antibiotic when you get a common cold.
12. nasal spray ['nezl̩ spre]	(n)噴鼻劑	例 A nasal spray can relieve the symptom of your stuffy nose.
13. antiviral drug ['æntɪ'vaɪrəl drʌg]	(n)抗病毒藥物；克流感藥物	例 You have to take antiviral drug four times a day.
14. inhale [ɪn'hel]	(v)吸入	例 We can drive to the country and inhale the fresh air.
15. asthma ['æzmə]	(n)氣喘病	例 Asthma is a lung disease that may lead to death.
16. pill [pɪl]	(n)藥丸	例 Sam took some pills when he had a fever.
17. vaccine ['væksin]	(n)疫苗	例 You should get a flu vaccine to prevent a seasonal flu.
18. trigger ['trɪgɚ]	(n)刺激物	例 Dust, tobacco smoke, air pollution, and pets are common triggers for asthma.
19. tobacco [tə'bæko]	(n)菸	例 Tobacco is bad for your health.

💡單字策略——故事串聯法

背單字的時候可以把單字編成一連串的故事，幫助記憶單字的意思。

感冒的時候一開始有 sore throat（喉嚨痛）跟 cough（咳嗽）→ 之後 fever（發燒）→ 最後 diarrhea（腹瀉）跟 vomiting（嘔吐）

試著把下列單字編成故事：sneeze, nasal spray, symptom, inhale, asthma, pill, vaccine, trigger, tobacco.

Reading

💡閱讀策略——圖表瀏覽技巧

如何看懂圖表呢？

當你看文章遇到圖表的時候，必須先看圖表上方的列（橫排）跟左方的欄（直排），例如：下面的文章每一欄（column）代表不同的疾病，每一列（row）告訴你每種疾病的徵兆、治療方法及預防措施。

Illnesses	Common cold	Seasonal flu (Influenza)	Asthma
Symptoms	Runny or stuffy nose; sore throat; sneeze; cough; mild headache and body aches.	Sudden fever; cough; sore throat; runny or stuffy nose; body aches; sometimes diarrhea and vomiting.	Breathlessness; chest tightness; nighttime or early morning coughing.
Treatment	Take antibiotics when they are needed. Get plenty of rest. Drink plenty of fluids. Use sore throat spray or nasal spray to relieve the symptoms.	Take antiviral drugs. Have plenty of rest. Drink a lot of fluids.	Inhale or breathe in asthma medicines. Take pills.
Prevention	Keep away from sick people. Eat a balanced diet. Exercise. Wash your hands often.	Get a flu vaccine. Wash your hands with soap and water. Keep away from sick people. Avoid crowds.	Remove the triggers in your environment, such as dust, tobacco smoke, air pollution, and pets.

Take care of yourself!

Made by Healthy Clinic

A. Read the notice made by Healthy Clinic and answer the following questions.

_____ 1. Which row tells you how to feel better or get well?

(A) illness　　(B) symptoms　　(C) treatment　　(D) prevention

_____ 2. Which column tells you about influenza?

(A) common cold　　(B) seasonal flu　　(C) asthma

_____ 3. Which column tells you how you feel if you get the illness?

(A) illness　　(B) symptoms　　(C) treatment　　(D) prevention

B. Answer the following questions based on the notice above.

1. If you catch a common cold, what should you do?

_____

2. If you want to prevent yourself from having flu, what should you do?

_____

3. What may be the symptoms of the asthma?

_____

Grammar

Modal auxiliaries（情態助動詞）：通常代表說話者的態度及傳達說話者態度的強弱程度，常用的情態助動詞有 can, could, had better, may, must, have to, should, ought to, would, will 等。

A. 某些情態助動詞可表示說話者認為某件事情是適宜的

1. You should wash your hands with soap and water before eating.
2. You ought to avoid crowds.

B. 某些情態助動詞表示說話者認為某件事情是必須的。

1. You must take the pills after each meal.
2. You have to take antiviral drugs.

Adverb of frequency（頻率副詞）：用來表達明確的頻率。例如："every day, twice a week, once a day" 等，通常放在句尾。

1. We should do exercise three times a week to maintain good health.
2. The doctor told me to use sore throat spray twice a day.
3. You ought to drink plenty of fluids several times a day.

Writing

A. Take a look at the Just Wondering Blog below and provide some advice for the following message.

Open Question

Just Wondering Blog

Jason77

I got a flu and sore throat~~

I got flu and sore throat last month, but I haven't seen a doctor or taken any medicine. It seems to be serious these days. Any suggestions?

Posted: Jan. 16

▣ Report Post

COLLAPSE MESSAGES

| Action Bar: | ↩ Reply | ⊘ Ignore Jason77 | ✉ Share This | ▤ More Posts By Jasont75 | ⊞ Add to Favorites |

Aqua77

Replying to: I got flu and sore throat~~

Usually you should get a full evaluation by your doctor at least once a year as a regular check. Since you have already got flu, you should consult your doctor sooner rather than later. Take care.

Posted: Jan. 19

| Action Bar: | ↩ Reply | ⊘ Ignore Jason77 | ✉ Share This | ▤ More Posts By Jasont75 | ⊞ Add to Favorites |

Sentence patterns you can use:

Suggestions	Frequency
◆ You should see a doctor.	◆ Once/twice/ three times + a day /a week / a month / a year
◆ Why don't you get plenty of rest?	
◆ You may take antiviral drugs to relieve your symptoms.	◆ ... hours per day
◆ You shouldn't have close contact with others.	
◆ How about trying the sore throat spray?	

Speaking

A.Call for registration. Find a partner to practice a telephone conversation for registration in the clinic. One plays a nurse who needs to complete the information below, and the other plays the patient. You may use the following sentence patterns.

Registration Record
ID number:
Register to see Dr.
Waiting number:
Date:
Time:

Sentence patterns you can use:

Nurse	Patient
🗣 Registration desk. May I help you?	🗣 I'd like to register to see Dr. ...
🗣 May I have your ID number?	🗣 My ID number is ...
🗣 Is this Mr./Ms./Mrs. ...?	🗣 Yes, that's right.
🗣 Mr./Ms./Mrs. .... Your waiting number is	🗣 OK! My number is ..., right?
🗣 Dr. ... will see you at room ... /Please come here at room...	🗣 Thank you for your help.

 數字的念法

　　當你唸數字的時候，要注意與金額的念法不同，只需將個別數字唸出來就好，不需要加上 hundred 及 thousand 這些字。如果遇到 0 可以唸成 zero 或是 o；如果遇到兩個同樣的數字可以使用 double 表示兩個的意思，triple 表示三個的意思，例如：253668 唸成 two five three double six eight; 288895 唸成 two triple eight nine five.

B. Orally read the following numbers

1. 558968
2. 744482
3. 123356
4. 855884
5. 650035

Listening

💡聽力策略──做筆記

聽數字的時候可以把聽到的數字，先轉化成阿拉伯數字，把阿拉伯數字寫下來，這樣可以將所聽到的訊息快速地變成可以理解的數字，並且加深對數字的印象。

Track 17

A. Listen to the time expressions and select the correct time below.

1. ☐ It's 5:35 / ☐ It's 3: 53
2. ☐ It's 8:40 / ☐ It's 4:08
3. ☐ It's 9:17 / ☐ It's 7:19

Track 18

B. Listen to the time expressions and write down the time below.

1. It's _____
2. It's _____

時間的表達方法

1. 在時間的表達中，可以用 a quarter（四分之一）這個字來講 15 分鐘，因為這個時間的時針跟分針剛好呈現四分之一的形式。

2. 表達 30 分以前的時間，使用 "after" 的講法，表示幾點過幾分。表達 30 分以後的時間，使用 "to" 的講法，表示再過幾分就幾點了。

例如：

9:15 A quarter after nine

9:20 Twenty minutes after nine

9:45 A quarter to ten

Track 19

C. Listen to the dialogue and answer the questions.

_____ 1. What time should Mr. Lin get to the clinic if his registration number is 19?

(A) 9: 15　　　(B) 9: 30　　　(C) 9:45　　　(D) 8:45

_____ 2. Mr. Lin won't get to the clinic until _____ this coming Friday.

 (A) 9: 00 (B) 9: 15   (C) 9:30   (D) 8:45

_____ 3. What time should Mr. Lin get to the clinic if his number is 36?

 (A) 9: 15 (B) 9: 30   (C) 9:45   (D) 8:45

ESP

Working as a nurse in a clinic

A nurse has to give instructions on how to take medicine.

A. Practice the expressions that are commonly used for giving instructions for medicine:

Nurse	Patient
🗣 Mr./Ms./Mrs.... These are all your drugs. 🗣 Please read the instructions on these medicines carefully. Do you have any questions? 🗣 The blue pack should be taken three times a day after each meal. 🗣 The red pack should be taken only when you get a fever. 🗣 Take the cough syrup once a day.	🗣 How should I take these drugs?
🗣 Take the whole dose for as many days as the doctor told you to. 🗣 Keep the drugs in a cool and dry place. 🗣 Antibiotics can cause allergic reactions or shortness of breath. 🗣 If you have these reactions, please come back to see the doctor.	🗣 Anything I should pay attention to? 🗣 Do these drugs have side effects? 🗣 What else should I know?

B. Work in pairs. Choose one situation. Use the expressions above to make a conversation with your partner.

 Situation 1: You are a nurse. Your patient asks you about medicine instruction.

 Situation 2: You are a patient. You ask about the side effects for the medicine.

Unit **7**

Living Green

Warm up

A. Do you know how to save energy? What are the DOs? What are the DON'Ts? Read the following examples. Write DOs or DON'Ts below each picture.

1. cut utility bills

DOs

2. reduce garbage

3. plug in plugs any time

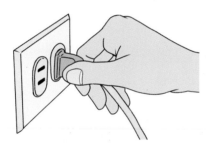

4. reuse paper

5. recycle plastic

6. grow one's own organic produce

7. shop for new stuff

8. carpool

9. use renewable energy

Vocabulary

💡單字策略——拆字法：以簡單字背困難字

　　有一些單字看似困難，但其實只要把它稍做拆解，便可以發現裡面有你認識的簡單字，如此一來便可以藉由簡單字來記憶困難字。例如：together = to get her。

　　在單字練習的單元中，例如 carpool 就可拆爲 car（車子）+ pool（共用資源）= 共乘。現在就用這個方法試著記憶下列單字吧。

1. reuse
2. recycle
3. renewable

其他練習：

1. plughole
2. waterfall
3. newscaster
4. blackmail
5. wetland

單字表

1. utility [ju'tɪlətɪ]	(n)公用事業（例如水、電等） (adj)公用事業的	例 I pay for utilities every two months. 例 Taiwan Power is a utility company.
2. bill [bɪl]	(n)帳單	例 Terry paid the bill yesterday.
3. reduce [rɪ'djus]	(v)減少	例 Everyone should reduce the use of energy.
4. reuse ['ri'juz]	(v)重複利用	例 Reusing paper will save a lot of trees.
5. plug [plʌg]	(n)插頭 (v)給…接通電源	例 Different kinds of plugs are used in different countries.
6. recycle [ri'saɪkl̩]	(v)使再循環	例 Plastic bottles need to be recycled.
7. organic [ɔr'gænɪk]	(adj)有機的	例 Many people prefer organic food nowadays.
8. produce ['prɑdus]	(n)農產品	例 Many organic vegetables can be found in the produce section.
9. stuff [stʌf]	(n)物品，東西	例 I left my stuff in the classroom.
10. carpool ['kɑr,pul]	(n)共乘制度 (v)汽車共乘	例 Mary joins the carpool to save money and energy. 例 We carpool to work.
11. renewable [rɪ'njuəbl̩]	(adj)可更新的	例 Wind is a type of renewable energy.
12. energy ['ɛnɚdʒɪ]	(n)能量	例 A car can't move without energy.

Reading

💡閱讀策略——透過文章的第一段來理解接下來的文章

　　文章的第一段常常會告訴讀者整篇文章的大意和重點，因此我們可以藉由文章的第一段來猜測並理解接下來的文章。所以文章的第一段是非常重要的。

A. Read the first paragraph of the passage "Saving the Earth and Your Money".

1. Do you know why saving the Earth can save your money?

2. Guess what the next paragraph will be about.

Saving the Earth and Your Money

Do you know saving the Earth can be a way of saving your money? If you do, you are probably doing it now. Many researchers have suggested that going green can save you a lot of money. For example, when you cut the utility bills by saving water, gas, and electric power, you are getting money saved. Driving less and taking public transportation are also good for the Earth as well as your wallet because you spend less on gas. As you know, gas is getting more and more expensive nowadays. So why don't you save the Earth? Many people are doing it now. Be creative and see what you can reduce and reuse to go green and save your money.

B. Read the rest of the passage. Check your guess.

There are several ways for you to save the Earth and your money. If you are taking most of the following actions. You are going green now.

Save on gas by walking, biking, carpooling, or taking public transportation.

Recycle paper, plastic products, and bottles.

Eat at least one vegetarian meal instead of meat each week.

Take a shower instead of a bath to save on your water bill.

Unplug plugs whenever possible.

Start an organic garden to grow your own vegetables and fruits.

Borrow books, CDs, and DVDs instead of buying them.

Exchange things with others, and reuse stuff instead of shopping.

Do you have any other creative ideas about living green? Share them with your friends and start doing it today!

C. Which of the above actions are you taking for going green? What are other creative ways that you can use to save the Earth? Write your answers in the box below. Then share them with your classmates.

Grammar

可數與不可數名詞（Countable and uncountable nouns）：

可數種類	不可數種類
◆人員（例如：a teacher）	◆液體（例如：water）
◆動物（例如：a dog）	◆食物（例如：bread）
◆物體（例如：a desk）	◆材料（例如：cotton）
◆衡量單位（例如：a mile）	◆活動（例如：travel）
	◆抽象的概念（例如：time）
	◆感覺（例如：happiness）

　　英文的可數名詞在沒有加定冠詞（**the, this, that, these, those**）或所有格（**my, your, his, her, our, their**等）的情況下，單數可數名詞就必須在其前面加 "**a (an)**"，而複數可數名詞則需於其字尾加上 "**s**"。至於不可數名詞則不需要在前面加上 "**a (an)**" 或於字尾加上 "**s**"。

A. 現在就依照上述可數與不可數名詞的種類，將下列單字歸類為可數與不可數名詞。如果是可數名詞，請幫它加上 "**a (an)**"。

assistant	tea	horse	wood	computer
dollar	rice	tennis	reality	anger

可數名詞	不可數名詞

B. 根據名詞可數與不可數概念在下列空格中填入正確的名詞型態。

1. A: Do you know that _____ (green tea) contains much catechin（兒茶素）？

   B: Oh, yes! I drink it almost everyday.

2. A: Do you have any _____ (information) about renewable energy?

   B: I know about solar energy and wind energy.

3. A: Did you buy _____ (newspaper) this morning?

   B: It's on the table!

4. A: I can't wait any longer.

   B: Come on! She's just two minutes late. Have some _____ (patience).

5. A: Do you have _____ (dollar) that I can borrow?

   B: Sure, there you go!

現在簡單式與進行式複習：

A. 你知道下列兩個句子中，那一個句子劃線部份使用現在簡單式（**present simple**）？那一個句子使用現在進行式（**present continuous**）呢？這兩個句子在句意上又有何不同呢？

1. When you cut utility bills by saving the energy and water you use around the house, you are getting more cash saved.

2. When you cut utility bills by saving the energy and water you use around the house, you get more cash saved.

現在簡單式（**present simple**）及現在進行式（**present continuous**）的使用：

Present Simple	Present Continuous
1.規律性或重覆的動作	1.現正發生的事情
例 I usually take public transportation.	例 Mark is reading a book now.
2.長期的狀態或事實	2.暫時的狀態或目前正在發展的趨勢
例 She lives in Taipei.	例 Lisa is working in Tokyo this year.
例 Water boils at 100 ℃.	例 Gas is getting more and more expensive nowadays

B. Choose the best response.

_____ 1. She _____ her report this week because it is due next Monday.

   (A) works on

   (B) is working on

   (C) work on

_____ 2. Giant is an international company that _____ bicycles.

   (A) is producing

   (B) produces

   (C) produce

_____ 3. Mary _____ on the phone right now.

  (A) talks

  (B) is talking

  (C) be talking

_____ 4. Humans _____ extreme weather during recent years.

  (A) are experiencing

  (B) experience

  (C) will experience

Writing

寫作策略──寫日誌（Keep a journal）

　　一個增進自我寫作能力的方式就是養成寫英文日誌的習慣。要如何幫助自己寫英文日誌呢？以下是一些技巧：

1. 選一個你可以專心的時間和地點。

2. 不需要求自己每天一定要寫一篇，重要的是保持常寫的習慣。

3. 開始寫的時候，先寫上日期，你也可以加入時間與地點。

4. 接著留一點空白以便寫完的時候可以給這一篇日誌一個標題。

5. 寫任何你可以想到的人、事、物。

6. 盡可能地把你想要表達的用英文寫出來，你也可以加上繪圖的方式來表達。

7. 為自己而寫，真心地表達。

　　當你回顧自己的日誌時，你一定會發現它的樂趣。

A. 練習寫下你的日誌。你可以回顧你目前所做的任何節省能源的事或是你未能做到節省能源的事。

　　例如：

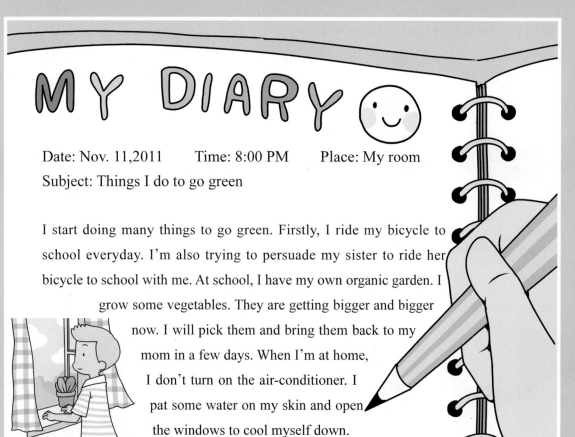

MY DIARY

Date: Nov. 11,2011   Time: 8:00 PM   Place: My room
Subject: Things I do to go green

I start doing many things to go green. Firstly, I ride my bicycle to school everyday. I'm also trying to persuade my sister to ride her bicycle to school with me. At school, I have my own organic garden. I grow some vegetables. They are getting bigger and bigger now. I will pick them and bring them back to my mom in a few days. When I'm at home, I don't turn on the air-conditioner. I pat some water on my skin and open the windows to cool myself down.

Speaking

A. Allen and Nicole respectively do something to save energy. You and your partner know only part of it. Can you help each other find out what Allen and Nicole do to go green?

Practice 1

Student A : Turn to page 73, you can see what Allen does to go green from the pictures. Answer Student B's questions according to the pictures.

Student B : Look at the pictures below. Ask Student A "Does Allen _____?" Circle the correct pictures.

Allen / Nicole (Circle the correct name)

Practice 2

Student B: Turn to page 74. You can see what Nicole does to live green from the pictures. Answer Student A's questions according to the pictures.

Student A : Look at the pictures above. Ask Student B "Does Nicole _____?" Circle the correct pictures.

Practice 3

Students A & B: Ask each other "What do you do to go green?" Write down each other's answers in the box below. Report your answers to the class.

Name:

Student A:

This is Allen.

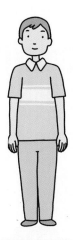

The following pictures show what he does to go green.

Answer Student B's qudestions.

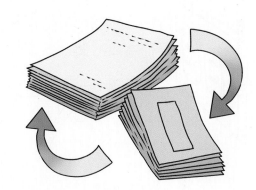

Student B:

This is Nicole.

The following pictures show what Nicole does to go green.

Answer Student A's qudestions.

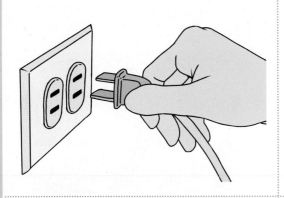

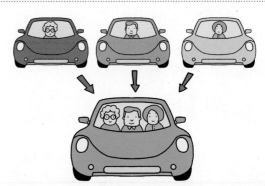

Listening

💡聽力策略──擷取重點

　　當我們聽一段談話時，例如演講、廣播等，我們必須要集中注意力，聽說話者的目的和一些特定的訊息（specific information），像是時間、地點等。但是由於這類談話通常比較長，很容易聽了後面卻忘了前面的訊息，因此，我們必需要把一些特定的訊息記下來。現在就試著聽關於日本綠能建設的談話，並把說話者的目的和一些特定訊息寫在下面的框框裡。

🎧 **Track 20**

A. **Listen to the talk. Take notes when you listen.**

```



```

B. **How many questions can you answer? Try to answer the questions according to the information you have noted down.**

_____ 1. What do Japanese do to reduce CO_2?

(A) to build a new airport.

(B) to collect snow.

(C) to close the airport.

_____ 2. How much energy is saved per year?

(A) 30%

(B) 40%

(C) 50%

_____ 3. How much CO_2 is reduced per year?

(A) 2000 tons

(B) 2100 tons

(C) 2200 tons

_____ 4. When was this process started?

(A) 1997

(B) 1998

(C) 1999

Track 21

C. **Listen again. Check your answers. (Remember to listen for the specific information.)**

ESP

A. 一位網友在 **YAHOO** 知識家發表了他對於再生能源（**renewable energy**）的疑問，你可以為他解答嗎？（你可以利用網路資源、書籍等）。

知識問題：Renewable energy?

發問者：Leslie（實習生 2 級）

發問時間：

2011-8-17 17:33:49

請各位大大幫我解答何謂 solar energy, wind energy, biomass energy, hydrogen energy, geothermal energy, and hydropower?

最佳解答：

回答者：

回答時間：

B. Match each type of energy with its correct definition.

Definitions:

1. solar energy _____

2. wind energy _____

3. biomass energy _____

4. hydrogen energy _____

5. geothermal energy _____

6. hydropower _____

a. Energy that uses plant or agricultural waste.

b. Energy that uses wind power.

c. Energy produced from flowing water.

d. Energy that makes use of sunlight.

e. Energy from the hot interior of the earth.

f. Energy that uses the lightest chemical element - H_2.

Note

H_2 是氫氣的化學符號，通常與氧結合，形成水 H_2O。

Unit

8

Banking

Warm Up

A. How many words can you recognize when you use the Automated Teller Machine to withdraw money?

Vocabulary

💡單字策略──字首字尾法

　　背單字的時候可以先看看是否有字首或字尾，字首可以決定單字的意思，而字尾可以決定單字的詞性，試著用這個方法猜猜看下面單字：

1. realistic → real 真的；實際的 -ic 形容詞 → 現實的
2. payment → pay 支付 -ment 名詞 → 支付；付款
3. impulse → im- 使成爲…；向…內 + pulse 拍打；震動；跳動 → 內心一直跳動 → 衝動
4. entertainment → entertain 使娛樂 -ment 名詞 → 餘興；娛樂；消遣
5. overindulge → over 超過 + indulge 使高興；沉迷；放縱 → 過於放縱
6. transportation → trans- 橫穿；通過 + port 港市 - tion 名詞 → 穿過很多港口城市 → 運輸；運送；運輸工具；交通車輛

單字表

1. tight [taɪt]	(adj)緊的；繃緊的	例 He complains about his tight schedule.
2. economy [ɪ'kɑnəmɪ]	(n)經濟	例 The government is trying to improve the country's economy.
3. realistic [rɪə'lɪstɪk]	(adj)現實的	例 We need to be realistic about the current situation.
4. budget ['bʌdʒɪt]	(n)預算；生活費	例 You need to keep your expense within your budget.
5. estimate ['ɛstə'met]	(v)估計	例 The cost is estimated to be ten thousand dollars a month.
6. payment ['pemənt]	(n)支付；付款	例 John made his last payment for his new house last month.
7. goal [gol]	(n)目的	例 Our goal is to save five thousand dollars per month
8. impulse ['ɪmpʌls]	(n)衝動；一時的念頭	例 You should try not to make decisions on impulse
9. purchase ['pɜˈtʃəs]	(v)購買	例 We used the money we saved to purchase a piano.

10. entertainment ['ɛntɚ'tenmənt]	(n)娛樂；消遣	例 For the entertainment of all the guests, the host sang a song after the dinner.
11. divide [də'vaɪd]	(n)劃分	例 I divide my income into different reasons for expense.
12. access ['æksɛs]	(v)接近；進入	例 Only a few of the employees can access to the secrets of this company.
13. prevent [prɪ'vɛnt]	(v)防止	例 One of the best ways to prevent you from colds is to exercise.
14. overindulge ['ovɚ-ɪn'dʌldʒ]	(v)放縱；溺愛	例 Parents should not overindulge their children.
15. transportation ['trænspɚ'teʃən]	(n)輸送；運送；交通工具	例 You may take public transportation to work to save some money.
16. thrift [θrɪft]	(n)節儉；節約	例 Many people here lead a life of thrift.

💡單字策略── 同義反義法

當妳在背單字的時候，可以先想一想是否之前有背過跟這個字意思相同或是想反的字。例如：之前有背過 sell 這個字，在這一課裡面看到的是 purchase 剛好是它的反義字。

A. 試著找出下面單字的同義或是反義字

    1. sell → 反義字 purchase

    2. idealistic → 反義字＿＿＿＿＿＿＿＿＿＿

    3. objective → 同義字 ＿＿＿＿＿＿＿＿＿＿

Reading

💡閱讀策略── 主題及主旨句預測技巧

當你看到文章時，要先看主標題及次標題，例如下面的文章就必須先看 "How to save your money" 這個主標題，然後從這個主題中可以預測到文章將會教我們存錢的方法。再來，就必須注意每段前面的粗體字 headings，看完 headings 可以大略猜到整段要講什麼。

A. Read the article and answer the following questions.

1. Look at the title of the article, what might the text be about?

   _____

2. Look at the headings of the following news report and guess what the author will talk about.

   (A) Develop a monthly budget: _____

   (B) Wait before you buy: _____

   (C) Limit spending: _____

   (D) Change your lifestyle: _____

How to Save your Money

In today's tight economy, people never have enough money. As an old saying goes "The more you make, the more you spend." Saving as much money as one can is an important issue for people nowadays. Several ways listed below can help you save money each month.

Develop a monthly budget. You should not just estimate your expenses each month. It is necessary that you take time to write down every dollar you have spent, such as payments on your rent or daily food. If you can develop a realistic budget, you can begin to set realistic goals to save money each month.

Wait before you buy. In order to avoid impulse purchases, it is important that you structure waiting time into your schedule. Wait for a period of time to control your impulse purchases. If you still want that item and you can afford it, then go ahead.

Limit spending. Put a limit on things, such as entertainment or drinks. It is critical that you divide money for entertainment into envelopes. Once your envelope is empty, it is suggested that there be no more dinners out. This means you keep enjoyment in your daily life, but prevent yourself from overindulging.

Change your lifestyle. Changing your life style will help you save money each month. It is recommended that you take public transportation, quit smoking and buy necessary items at thrift stores to save money little by little each month.

_____

B. Look back at your predictions and check if they are correct.

Grammar

Subjunctive verbs（意志動詞）：意志動詞要表達的是強調重要性或是急迫性。

---

1. It is necessary that you take time to write down every dollar you have spent, such as payments on your rent or daily food.

2. It is important that he structure waiting time into his schedule.

3. It is critical that you divide money for entertainment into envelopes.

4. It is recommended that she take public transportation, quit smoking and buy some necessary items at thrift stores.

A. 請依照上面的例句寫出使用意志動詞的公式

公式：It is necessary/important/critical/suggested + that + ＿＿＿＿＿＿＿＿＿

當你使用意志動詞時，that 子句裡面的動詞需要使用原形動詞。句子裡面原來有 should 用來加強子句中動詞的語氣，但是 should 這個字通常被省略。

常用的意志動詞有 ask, demand, insist, propose, recommend, request 等。

使用意志動詞時，可以用下列公式來幫助記憶：

公式：主詞 + 意志動詞 + that + 主詞 + (should) + 原 V

B. Choose the correct answer to complete the following sentences.

_____ 1. The teacher demands that we _____ on time.

　　(A) are　　　　(B) were　　　　(C) be　　　　(D) are going to

_____ 2. I insisted that he _____ me the money.

　　(A) pays　　　(B) paid　　　　(C) has paid　　(D) pay

_____ 3. I recommended that she _____ to the concert.

　　(A) doesn't go　(B) goes　　　(C) not go　　　(D) went

_____ 4. I suggested that you _____ a good student.

　　(A) are　　　　(B) were　　　　(C) be　　　　(D) are going to

_____ 5. It is important that they _____ the truth.

　　(A) tells　　　(B) told　　　　(C) tell　　　　(D) are told

Writing

A. **Share your opinions about how to save money. Take a look at the money saving Blog below and provide three suggestions for the following message. You may use the sentence patterns below.**

 Judy

Edit Friends
Account Settings
Privacy Settings
Application Settings
Credits Balance
Help Center
Logout

Search Messages

New Message

Money saving

Between Clover and You

 Judy March 6 at 10:53am

I want to save more money each month~~ I earn twenty thousand NT dollars per month. I intend to buy a new car next year. How can I save more money?

 Clover March 6 at 11:00am

I can share some helpful tips with you. I suggest that you collect coupons for your daily consumption, such as coupons for restaurants, supermarkets, department stores and the like. Also, I recommend that you avoid unplanned shopping. Finally, it is important you stop spending money on beverages and start to carry your own water bottle. I hope that these tips can help you save as much money as you can.

Reply:

Reply

Back to MessagesEdit Subscriptions

Sentence Patterns

◆ I advise that you ...

◆ I recommend that you...

◆ I suggest that you...

◆ It is important that you...

◆ It is essential that you ...

Speaking

💡口說策略——使用開頭語爭取時間

　　表達自我意見時，可以先用表達自我意見的片語，例如 "in my opinion" 等，一方面告訴對方這是你自己的看法，另外一方面可以為自己爭取思考下面要講甚麼的時間，這樣可以讓你的口語表達更為順暢。

A. CJC broadcast has a call-in program. What are your opinions on saving money? Call in and express your opinions. You may use the sentence patterns below.

Sentence patterns you can use.:

How to express your opinions?	Opinions
🗣 I think ...	🗣 You should go around the city by bike instead of car.
🗣 For me ...	
🗣 As far as I am concerned, ...	🗣 You ought to cook at home instead of eating out.
🗣 I consider ...	
🗣 In my opinion, ...	
🗣 I believe ...	
🗣 Take ... for example, ...	

Listening

💡聽力策略——聽表達順序的字詞

　　當你聽很多資訊的時候，需要注意裡面表達順序的字詞，例如：at first, secondly, thirdly, next, then, finally 等字眼，它們可以幫助你把許多資訊排列整理成條列式，幫助你很快地抓到文本的重點所在。

🎧 **Track 22**

A. Listen to the following reports for the opinions and take notes on each of them.

1. Sequencing word: ＿＿＿＿＿＿　　Opinion: ＿＿＿＿＿＿＿＿＿

2. Sequencing word: ＿＿＿＿＿＿　　Opinion: ＿＿＿＿＿＿＿＿＿

3. Sequencing word: ＿＿＿＿＿＿　　Opinion: ＿＿＿＿＿＿＿＿＿

🎧 **Track 23**

B. Listen to the following dialogue and choose the correct answer.

＿＿＿ 1. What is the purpose for the call? To express the opinions on ＿＿＿＿＿＿.

(A) saving money

(B) using credit card

(C) buying things

(D) the interest rate of savings account.

＿＿＿ 2. What is the first reason why the caller doesn't want to have a credit card? A credit card ＿＿＿＿＿＿.

(A) makes her purchase out of control.

(B) brings extra interest charges for minimum payment.

(C) brings her extra fees when the payment is delayed.

(D) fraud is a danger if the card gets stolen.

＿＿＿ 3. What is the second reason why the caller doesn't want to have a credit card? A credit card ＿＿＿＿＿＿.

(A) makes her purchase out of control.

(B) brings extra interest charges for minimum payment.

(C) brings her extra fees when the payment is delayed.

(D) fraud is annoying when the card is stolen.

_____ 4. What is the third reason why the caller doesn't want to have a credit card? A credit card _____.

(A) makes her purchase out of control.

(B) brings extra interest charges for minimum payment.

(C) brings her extra fees when the payment is delayed.

(D) fraud is a danger when the card gets stolen.

ESP

Working as a bank receptionist in a bank: A bank teller has to help customers to fill in forms.

A. Practice the expressions that are commonly used for form-filling instructions:

Customer	Bank teller
Open a new account	
🗨 I'd like to open a new account. 🗨 What document should I prepare?	🗨 Sure. May I have your valid passport and visa? 🗨 Have you brought any other documents for further identification, such as resident visa, driver's license, or health IC card? 🗨 Please fill in the application form here.
Deposit money	
🗨 I'd like to deposit some money. 🗨 Do I need to fill in any forms?	🗨 Certainly, have you brought your passbook? 🗨 Yes, you need to fill in the deposit form. 🗨 Please fill in the date, your name, your account number, and the amount you would like to deposit.
Withdraw money	
🗨 Excuse me. I'd like to withdraw some money. 🗨 What kind of form should I fill in?	🗨 No problem, may I have your passbook and withdrawal forms? 🗨 You need to fill in the form for withdrawal. 🗨 Please fill in the date, your name, your account number, and the amount you would like to withdraw. 🗨 Please key in your code for withdrawal here.

B. Work in pairs. Choose one situation. Use the expressions above to make a conversation.

Situation 1: You are a bank teller. Your customer asks you how to open a new account.

Situation 2: You are a customer. You ask how to deposit and withdraw your money.

Unit **9**

Common Courtesy

Warm Up

A. What do you think of the following behavior?

Reading

💡閱讀策略──文章瀏覽技巧

　　當你看文章的時候，要如何快速的閱讀呢？首先，你可以先看標題及次標題。例如：下面的文章中，你要先瀏覽主標題 "How to have common courtesy" 這個標題表示這篇文章要講的是如何做到一般禮儀。之後，瀏覽第一段，第一段通常會介紹整篇的內容。再來，先瀏覽次標題，次標題中提到 "At home"、"On the Road" 及 "At work" 表示會介紹家裡、路上及工作場合的一般禮節等。最後，瀏覽每個段落的第一句，每段的第一句代表著該段的內容會講甚麼，現在就趕快用瀏覽技巧找找文章要告訴你怎麼做個有禮節的人。

A. Read the article "How to Have Common Courtesy" from the website and answer the following questions

_____ 1. What is the main purpose of the article?

(A) To teach people how to think of others at home

(B) To teach people how to drive on the road

(C) To teach people how to work with others

(D) To teach people how to be courteous to others

_____ 2. Which paragraph tells you about good driving manners?

      (A) 1   (B) 2   (C) 3   (D) 4

_____ 3. Which paragraph indicates how to be courteous in business situations?

      (A) 1   (B) 2   (C) 3   (D) 4

_____ 4. Which paragraph gives a general introduction to the whole article?

      (A) 1   (B) 2   (C) 3   (D) 4

How to Have Common Courtesy

Courtesy is a kind of behavior that shows respect to others. Here are some tips on using common courtesy in different situations. Learning these tips can help us get along better with others.

At Home

Being courteous at home means that we should consider helping others from time to time instead of thinking of ourselves first. We should try doing housework without being asked and giving up bad habits. Bad habits may not get better unless we are aware of them. If we pick up bad habits, they may become normal and it is hard for us to get rid of them.

On the Road

Driving with bad manners can be annoying. We should not treat others discourteously on the road when we are in a hurry. We should use the turn signal and take more than one glance behind us to check if the way is clear before switching lanes. We should avoid occupying two spaces in the parking lot. We should be courteous to other people's property and avoid banging our door against other people's cars.

At work

Holding the elevator for others is a good gesture. Pushing the floor buttons is an even better one. Holding the door for those who want to come in or go out is very courteous too. In business situations, we always need to be courteous by saying "hello" and "goodbye." If we are on the phone, we should not hang up on the one we are talking to because this type of discourtesy may leave a bad impression on the other end.

B. Read the article again. Write "T" for true and "F" for false according to the information in the text.

_____ 1. One way to be courteous at home is to do something without being asked.

_____ 2. One way to be courteous on the road is to use signals for the people driving behind you.

_____ 3. One way to be courteous at work is to avoid holding the elevator and other doors.

Vocabulary

💡單字策略——字首法

　　試著將下面的單字拆開，你可以從單字的字首判斷單字意思

1. respectful = re- 再一次 + spec- 看 + -ful 充滿的 = 一再一再看的 → 充滿尊重的；恭敬的；尊敬的；尊重人的

2. discourteous = dis- 相反；否定；不 + court 殷勤 + -ous 形容詞 → 不殷勤的 → 失禮的；不禮貌的

3. avoid = a- 沒有；缺乏；不 + void 空出；空隙；退出 → 避免

4. discourtesy = dis- 相反；否定；不 + court 殷勤 + -y 名詞 → 不殷勤 → 失禮；不禮貌

5. impression = im- 向…內 + press 壓 + -sion 名詞 = 向內壓 → 印象深刻

單字表

1.courtesy ['kɝtəsɪ]	(n)禮貌；殷勤；好意	例 Common courtesy is an important issue that everyone should know about.
2.respect [rɪ'spɛkt]	(n)敬重；尊敬	例 People in Taiwan usually show their respect to their teachers.
3.courteous ['kɝtiəs]	(adj) 殷勤的；謙恭的；有禮貌的	例 The boy is always courteous to everyone.
4.consider [kən'sɪdɚ]	(v)考慮；細想	例 John is considering changing his major.
5.normal ['nɔrml]	(adj)正常的；正規的；標準的	例 Making mistakes is normal for people.
6.manner ['mænɚ]	(n)方式；方法；禮貌；規矩；習慣	例 The gentleman shows his good manners by opening the car door for his elders.
7.annoying [ə'nɔɪɪŋ]	(adj)討厭的；惱人的；使人煩惱的	例 Speaking loudly in a museum is annoying behavior.
8.discourteously [dɪs'kɝtiəslɪ]	(adv)失禮地；不禮貌地；粗魯地	例 That man discourteously entered my room without permission.
9.glance [glæns]	(n)一瞥；大略的看過	例 That store seems quite interesting, so let's take a glance at it.

10. lane [len]	(n)小路；巷；弄	例 The car is blocking the narrow lane, so we should try the other side.
11. avoid [ə'vɔɪd]	(v)避免	例 You should avoid interrupting others while they are in a meeting.
12. occupy ['akjə'paɪ]	(v)佔（時間；空間）；佔用；住	例 Occupying the reserved seat is discourteous.
13. property ['prapə-tɪ]	(n)財產；資產；所有物	例 This apartment is the property of an old lady.
14. bang [bæŋ]	(v)猛擊；猛撞；撞擊	例 That drunk man banged the door against the house
15. discourtesy [dɪs'kɜ-təsɪ]	(n)無禮；粗魯的言行	例 The discourtesy shown to your friend is unforgivable.
16. elevator ['ɛlə'vetə-]	(n)電梯；升降機	例 Smoking is forbidden in the elevator.
17. gesture ['dʒɛstʃə-]	(n)姿勢；手勢；姿態	例 Waving hands is a gesture for calling somebody.
18. button ['bʌtn̩]	(n)按鈕	例 Push the button and the door will open.
19. impression [ɪm'prɛʃən]	(n)印象	例 You should try to make a good impression on your employer.
20. display [dɪ`sple]	(v)陳列；展出	例 The watches are displayed on the table so that the customers can try them one by one.
21. handicapped [`hændɪ,kæpt]	(adj)有生理缺陷的；殘障的	例 We should not park our car in a handicapped parking lot.
22. gossip [`gasəp]	(n)閒話；聊天；流言蜚語	例 According to the report, two-thirds of all conversation is gossip.
23. compliment [`kampləmənt]	(v)讚美；恭維；祝賀	例 Complimenting people may help others feel confident.

試著將下面的單字拆開，你可以從單字的字尾判斷單字的詞性及意思

1. courteous = court 殷勤 + e + -ous 形容詞 → 殷勤的；有禮貌的

2. courtesy = court 殷勤 + e + -y 名詞 → 殷勤；有禮貌；好意

3. normal = norm 基準；規範 + -al 形容詞 → 正常的；正規的；標準的

4. annoying = annoy 惹惱；使生氣 + -ing 形容詞 → 討厭的；惱人的

5. elevator = elevate 舉起；抬起 + (-e) + -or 名詞（人；物；機）→ 電梯

6. probably = probable 可能的 + (-e) + -ly 副詞 → 可能地

Grammar

Using gerund as a noun phrase（動名詞當主詞）：動名詞當主詞使用的時候，通常被視為不可數名詞。

1. Learning these tips can help us get along better with others.

2. Driving with bad manners can be very annoying.

3. Being courteous at home means that we should consider others from time to time instead of thinking of ourselves first.

4. Pushing the floor buttons for others is even a nicer one.

5. Holding the door for those who want to come in or go out is very courteous too.

6. Holding the elevator is a nice gesture.

你能寫出動名詞當主詞的公式嗎？

公式：_____ can be / is...

The gerund should be used after prepositions（介系詞後加動名詞）：介系詞後面如有動詞時，動詞需改為動名詞形式。

1. We should try doing housework without being asked and giving up bad habits.

2. In business situations, we always need to be courteous by saying "hello" and "goodbye."

The gerund should be used after certain verbs（加動名詞的動詞）：某些動詞後面如果加上第二個動詞，第二個動詞常用動名詞形式，例如：consider, suggest, mention, enjoy, finish, keep, avoid, postpone, delay, stop, appreciate.

1. We should <u>consider helping</u> others from time to time instead of thinking of ourselves first.

2. We should <u>avoid occupying</u> two spaces in the parking lot.

3. We should <u>avoid banging</u> our door into other people's cars.

A. Choose the correct answer for the following sentences.

_____ 1. Do not invest without _____ either me or one of the managers.

    (A) consult   (B) to consult   (C) consulting   (D) consulted

_____ 2. Turning off all the lights _____ the responsibility for all the employees in this company.

    (A) is   (B) are   (C) have been   (D) were

_____ 3. _____ new employees is the first consideration in the new firm.

    (A) Hire   (B) Hired   (C) Be hired   (D) Hiring

_____ 4. We consider _____ you some other models of this new product.

    (A) to recommend   (B) recommending   (C) recommended   (D) recommend

_____ 5. We appreciate your contributions and look forward to _____ from you soon.

    (A) hear   (B) be heard   (C) heard   (D) hearing

Writing

A. The following strips show an embarrassing situation. Complete each sentence by using the following verbs: parked, banged, has already occupied, argued.

1

(A) Chris _____ his scooter in a parking space when he was rushing for a job interview.

2

(B) A car driver wanted to park his car in this space, but he found that a scooter _____ this space.

3

(C) The car driver was angry and _____ the door against the scooter. This made Chris angry, so he argued with the car driver.

4

(D) When Chris stepped into the office for the job interview, he found that the car driver that he _____ with was the employer.

B. **Comment on the behavior for each picture and then give Chris some advice by using the verbs like "consider, recommend, avoid, finish, keep, quit" to practice using gerund. Make four sentences to give comment and advice. You may use the following sentence patterns.**

Sentence Patterns

Comment	Your advice
◆ Parking the car/motorcycle in the ...	◆ Chris should avoid ...
◆ Occupying the parking lot ...	◆ I recommend ...
◆ Banging the door ...	◆ Chris should ...
◆ Attending the job interview ...	◆ I consider ...

For picture 1: _____

_____

_____

_____

For picture 2:_____

_____

_____

For picture 3:_____

_____

_____

For picture 4:_____

_____

_____

Speaking

A. **Give praise generously: it's FREE! Find a partner and take turns to compliment each other on a good job. You may use the following sentence patterns.**

Sentence patterns:

How to express your compliment	How to respond others' compliments
🔊 I really appreciate your ...	🔊 Thank you.
🔊 You are really a good ...	🔊 Thank you for your compliment.
🔊 You really did a perfect job.	🔊 That's very kind of you to say that.
🔊 You are capable of ...	🔊 That's very nice of you to say that.
🔊 You are a very capable ...	🔊 I am glad to hear that.
🔊 You have a great capacity for ...	🔊 I am pleased to hear that.

Note 如何接受他人讚美

當你聽到別人對你的讚美時,通常不用 "no" 等負面表達反應。而是會欣然接受,說句 "thank you" 或 "thanks for your compliment" 這些比較正面的回應。

Listening

💡聽力策略——聽關鍵字及做筆記

　　聽的時候可以試著把重點寫下來，一般而言，重點大部分是在名詞或是動詞，試著注意聽這些字之後寫下來，可以幫助你記憶一些重要的資訊。

 Track 24

A. Listen to the following statements and fill in the blanks.

1. If someone is new to the company or neighborhood, _____ yourself and assisting them can show your kindness. Being sincere and giving a little personal _____ can make the newcomer feel welcome. _____ a basket of food is a good way to welcome your new neighbors.

2. _____ of someone else shows courtesy. Displaying this in your everyday behavior, such as_____ the door or a car door for others.

3. Putting _____ items back is a nice gesture. Everything should have its own _____; if you take it out, it's courteous to put it back so that the next person can find it when he or she needs it!

Track 25

B. Listen to the following statements and choose the correct answer

_____ 1. According to the passage, how can we show our driving courtesy?

　　(A) Avoiding blocking the exit.

　　(B) Taking few minutes to drive

　　(C) Shifting among lanes quickly

　　(D) Changing lanes without signalling.

_____ 2. According to the passage, what can we do to show our courtesy?

　　(A) Avoiding blocking the exit

　　(B) Supporting the disabled

　　(C) Gossiping with the handicapped

　　(D) Finding interests for the elderly

_____ 3. According to the passage, if we don't have something nice to say, what should we do?

(A) Complimenting others

(B) Helping others

(C) Saying nothing

(D) Inspiring others

_____ 4. According to the passage, what should we do to encourage others to do their best?

(A) Keeping gossip to ourselves

(B) Helping others when they need us

(C) Complimenting others all the time

(D) Inspiring others when they need it

ESP

Working as a sales representative, you need to be courteous when you receive customers.

A. Practice the expressions that are commonly used for receiving customers.

Sales representative	Customer
Greeting and Business Card Exchange	
🎤 Welcome to our company.	🎤 Thank you, Mr./Ms. ... .
🎤 We have been expecting you.	🎤 Here is my card.
🎤 I'm ... / My name is	🎤 I am responsible for ... in our company.
🎤 I am a sales representative in the ... department.	🎤 Thanks for letting me visit your company.
	🎤 I am glad to come here.
🎤 Please accept my card.	🎤 It's my honor to visit your company.
🎤 I am in charge of the ... department.	
🎤 I have been working here for	
Introducing your company	

🎤 Please allow me to introduce our company.	🎤 It was really a good idea to come here.
🎤 Our firm has been established for … .	🎤 When was your company established?
🎤 We deal with … .	🎤 What do you produce?
🎤 We produce … .	🎤 Can you show me your … ?
🎤 It's my pleasure to show you some of our new products.	🎤 May I take a look at your …?
🎤 I'm sure you'll be interested in these high-quality goods.	🎤 Would you mind … ?
🎤 Here you can see the complete process.	🎤 Would you mind if I … ?

Ending the conversation	
🎤 I am really glad you could come.	🎤 I appreciate your kindness.
🎤 It's been very pleasant talking to you.	🎤 Thank you for your time.
🎤 Thank you for taking time to visit us.	🎤 Thank you for inviting me here.

B. Work in pairs. Choose one situation. Use the expressions above.

Situation 1:

You are a sales representative from ABC company and your employer asks you to visit DEF company. You need to greet and introduce yourself to the sales representative of DEF company.

Situation 2:

You are a sales representative of a stationery company. Your employer invites a potential customer to come to visit your company. You need to introduce your company to the customer.

Unit

10

Housing

Warm Up

A. Match the picture with its English name

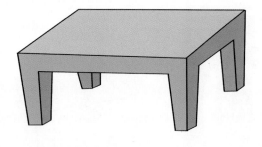

1. sofa

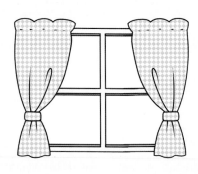

2. coffee table

3. rug

4. curtain

B. Draw a picture of your room and identify the furniture or other decorations in it.

C. Match the word with its item shown on the picture below.

1. _____ 4. _____ 7. _____ 10. _____

2. _____ 5. _____ 8. _____ 11. _____

3. _____ 6. _____ 9. _____ 12. _____

end table	fireplace	lamp	coffee table
curtain	rug	floor	throw pillow
sofa	painting	loveseat	armchair

Reading

單字猜測技巧

　　當你看文章的時候，如果有遇到不會的單字先不要急著查字典，請根據下列步驟並且利用上下文的線索，來猜測單字可能的意思。

1. 例如："I like a feeling of space; therefore, there is no unnecessary furniture" 的句子裡面 "unnecessary" 這個字是沒有學過的單字。首先，先判斷這個單字可能的詞性："unnecessary" 可能的詞性是「形容詞」，用來修飾 "furniture" 這個名詞。再來，從單字的字首拆開，看能不能猜出可能的意思。"un-" 代表「否定」的意思，"necessary" 代表「需要」的意思，因此，這個字可能的意思是「不需要」。

2. 如果沒有辦法用字根字首來猜測的單字，就需要使用最靠近這個單字的鄰近線索字或詞來猜出這個單字。以下介紹幾個最常見的線索：

線索1："For example"

例句：I like a feeling of space; therefore, there is no unnecessary furniture. For example, there are a sofa, a coffee table, and an armchair.

解說：如果看不懂這句話的 "furniture" 這個字，就可以從後面 "for example" 的舉例物品來推敲。可以猜出 "furniture" 就是「家用產品」或是「傢俱」的意思。

線索2："and"

例句：There are a sofa, a coffee table, and an armchair.

解說：如果看不懂這句話的 "armchair" 這個字，就可以從 "and" 前面的東西來猜。它們應該都是屬於同一種類的物品，可能猜出 "armchair" 就是「桌椅類」的意思。

線索3："because, so that, so"

例句：I put a throw pillow on my sofa so that I can feel more comfortable when I lie down for a rest.

解說：如果看不懂這句話的 "throw pillow" 這個字，就可以從 "on my sofa" 以及 "so that" 這兩個線索字來猜測。這個東西放在沙發上面，而且會讓你躺在沙發上感覺很舒服，可以猜出 "throw pillow" 就是「枕頭之類的柔軟物品」的意思。

How to Decorate My Living Room?

第1行   I want to decorate my living room to make it more stylish. The following description is about my living room.

    I like to stay in my living room. It is a medium-sized room which has one large window with curtains. Although it is not a beautiful room, it is very comfortable. I like a feeling of 第5行 space; therefore, there is no unnecessary furniture. For example, there are a sofa, a coffee table, a loveseat, a fireplace, an armchair, and an end table. The sofa is against the window and a coffee table is in front of my sofa. Under the coffee table is the rug. The loveseat is positioned left side of the coffee table in the corner. The fireplace against the wall is next to the loveseat. The armchair is positioned at the right side of the coffee table. An end table is set at the left side 第10行 of the armchair.

    As for the decoration, I painted my wall in white to make it light. The curtains are deep purple; the sofa is light blue; the rug is orange; the armchair is light green, and the loveseat is pink. Most furniture was either given by my friends or bought second-hand from flea markets. I painted tables dark brown because they were old and shabby. After my painting, they look as 第15行 good as new now. The lamp is on the end table which provides me some light when I lie down and read novels. I put a throw pillow on my sofa so that I can feel more comfortable when I lie down for a rest. I also have a landscape painting on the wall. I love it because it brings me feeling of relaxing.

    The living room has been the same ever since I moved into the house. I want to redecorate 第20行 and consider buying some new furniture. If you have any new ideas, please leave your message on my housing blog.

A. Read the article and answer the following questions.

_____ 1. hat does the word "loveseat" in line 6 mean?

    (A) A kind of room

    (B) A kind of furniture

    (C) A kind of space

    (D) A kind of place

_____ 2. What does the phrase "flea market" in line 13 mean?

    (A) A place where we can buy new things

    (B) A place where we can buy used things

    (C) A place where we can buy expensive things

    (D) A place where we can buy fresh things

_____ 3. What does the word "shabby" in line 14 mean?

    (A) worn

    (B) shining

    (C) shaped

    (D) odd

_____ 4. What does the word "landscape" in line 17 mean?

    (A) scenario

    (B) landmark

    (C) landholder

    (D) scene

Vocabulary

💡單字策略──拆字法

1. unnecessary → un- 否定 + necessary 需要的 → 不需要的

2. coffee table → coffee 咖啡 + table 桌子 → 放咖啡或茶的桌子 → 茶几

3. loveseat → love 戀愛 + seat 座位 → 戀愛情人座椅 → 雙人椅

4. armchair → arm 手臂 + chair 椅子 → 扶手椅

5. throw pillow → throw 丟 + pillow 枕頭 → 可以丟來丟去的枕頭 → 抱枕

6. end table → end 盡頭 + table 桌子 → 放在盡頭的桌子 → 小茶几

7. fireplace → fire 火 + place 地方 → 有火的地方 → 壁爐

8. painting → paint 繪畫 + -ing 名詞 → 繪畫的作品

單字表

1. decorate ['dɛkə,ret]	(n)裝飾	例 The designer decorated the hat with flowers.
2. description [dɪ'skrɪpʃən]	(n)描述	例 According to descriptions made by the witness, the robbery happened around 10 o'clock last night.
3. unnecessary [ʌn'nɛsə,sɛrɪ]	(adj)不需要的	例 In order to make a successful speech, you need to avoid unnecessary wordings.
4. coffee table ['kɔfɪ'tebḷ]	(n)茶几	例 We usually put some magazines on the coffee table.
5. sofa ['sofə]	(n)沙發	例 The sofa is next to a plant.
6. rug [rʌg]	(n)小地毯	例 We may decorate the floor with a rug.
7. loveseat ['lʌvsit]	(n)雙人椅	例 You can find loveseats in that furniture store.
8. fireplace ['faɪr,ples]	(n)壁爐	例 During winter, the cat often sleeps beside the fireplace
9. armchair ['ɑrm,tʃɛr]	(n)扶手椅	例 If you want to rest arms when you sit, you may buy an armchair.
10. position [pə'zɪʃən]	(v)放置	例 The woman positioned the armchair in front of the fireplace.
11. end table ['ɛnd,tebḷ]	(n)小茶几	例 The end table is positioned in the corner of this room.
12. decoration [,dɛkə'reʃən]	(n)裝飾	例 During Christmas season, people like to put decorations on Christmas trees.
13. curtain ['kɝtṇ]	(n)窗簾	例 Can you draw the curtains for me?
14. flea market ['fli,mɑrkɪt]	(n)跳蚤市場	例 We can see many second-hand or cheap goods in the flea market.
15. shabby ['ʃæbɪ]	(adj)破舊的	例 The old building looks shabby.
16. lamp [læmp]	(n)燈	例 There is usually a lamp on each desk in the library.

17. novel [`nɑvl]	(n)小說	例 The Lord of the Rings is a famous novel.
18. throw pillow [`θro,pɪlo]	(n)抱枕	例 There are two throw pillows on the sofa.
19. landscape [`lænd,skep]	(n)風景	例 From the top of the mountain, we can see the beautiful landscape of the field.
20. painting [`pentɪŋ]	(n)水彩畫	例 The landscape painting is hanged on the wall in our living room.

Grammar

Preposition（介系詞）：用來表示佈置、方位、位置。

你可以使用圖像來幫助自己記住介系詞在空間及方位上的使用。

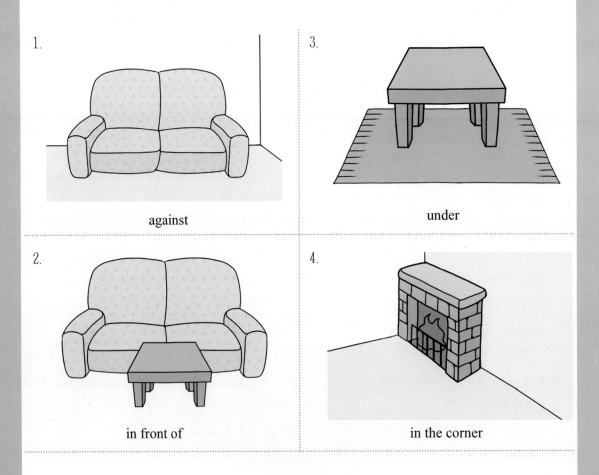

1. against

3. under

2. in front of

4. in the corner

5.

next to

6.

on

A. 根據下列句子在空格中畫出東西之間的佈置跟方位。

1. The sofa is <u>against</u> the window.

2. A coffee table is <u>in front of</u> the sofa.

3. <u>Under</u> the end table is the rug.

4. The loveseat is <u>in the corner</u>.

5. The fireplace is <u>next to</u> the loveseat.

6. The throw pillow is <u>on</u> the armchair.

1.	3.	5.
2.	4.	6.

Writing

💡寫作策略——列下寫作要點

當你在寫作之前，可以先把你要寫的幾個要點分成幾個重點列下來，如同下面 outline 所列，把要寫的東西分成四個段落，依照這四個要點再加以說明及舉例。

A. Describe the picture that you draw in the warm-up section of this unit, by using the following outline.

Outline

Paragraph 1: General introduction
Paragraph 2: The size of your room (small / medium / large) and the main furniture
Paragraph 3: The decoration and your favorite items
Paragraph 4: Conclusion and summary

Speaking

A. Describe Tony's room below.

Prepositions you can use:

How to describe location						
🗣 next to	🗣 beside	🗣 beneath	🗣 below	🗣 under	🗣 on	🗣 in
🗣 in the corner	🗣 against	🗣 behind	🗣 in front of	🗣 in back of		

B. Describe the interior arrangement of the mansion below.

💡口說策略 ── 空間描述

　　當你在描述圖片的時候，應該要有順序性，可採用順時鐘或逆時鐘的方式來描述，或是由內而外或由外而內的方式來表達，這樣可以幫助聽眾快速了解整個圖片或是物品的配置。

Listening

💡聽力策略 ── 圖片預測技巧

　　做聽力練習的時候，如果題目有提供圖片，應該先審閱圖片中的訊息，並且在聽文本之前，先預測可能會出現的單字有哪些。聽到文本的時候應該特別注意剛剛預測的單字是否真的出現。

🎵 **Track 26**

A. Listen to the descriptions and check the correct picture according to the text.

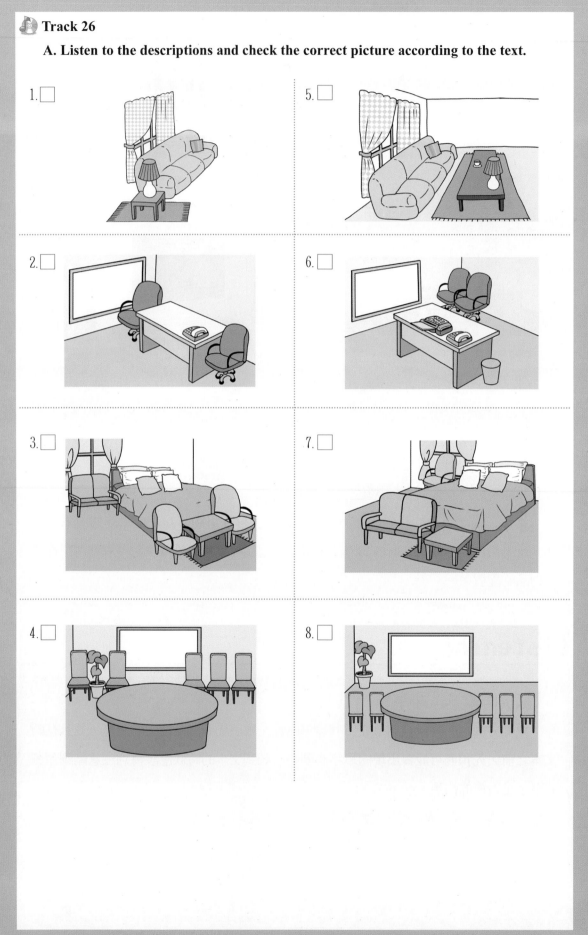

1. ☐

5. ☐

2. ☐

6. ☐

3. ☐

7. ☐

4. ☐

8. ☐

ESP

💡專業文章閱讀策略——快速知道專業文章的各段主旨

　　閱讀專業文章的時候，如何很快速地知道各段落的主旨呢？首先，可以先看看有沒有圖片，從圖片的線索可以略知一二。再來，閱讀每一段的第一句大概就會告訴你這一整段約略的內容。最後，很快地瀏覽整個段落，找出相關的線索字，再將這些線索字聯結出可能的大意。例如：下面的專業文章中，介紹不同的室內裝潢主題。第一段介紹整篇文章的大意之後，接下來分段介紹各個主題的要點。第二段的第一句話文章寫著 "Many people paint their walls in white, ivory, or light gray." 等有關於牆壁的粉刷顏色。而在整個段落之中出現了 "color"、"painting"、"one wall"、"focus wall"、"paint colors" 等重點字，所以這個段落的主旨就是 "Wall Paint"。現在從第三段開始由你來練習看看，是不是能夠很快地找到它的主旨。

A. 依照各段的主旨句以及段落中的重點字，從以下主旨選單中，選出各個段落的主旨。

　　主旨：**Organization**

　　　　　Decorating Styles

　　　　　Wall Paint

　　　　　Color Schemes

Interior Design

Interior Design includes furniture, fabrics, colors, textures and styles that make your home look better. There are many things that you need to consider when you want to decorate your house and it can be an overwhelming process. In addition to costs, furniture and decorative elements, you also need to choose color schemes, decorating themes, and different styles of interior arrangement.

Wall Paint

Many people paint their walls in white, ivory, or light gray. If you like the color, you don't have to change it. However, if you are afraid of changing your walls into new colors, try to paint just one wall; that is, a focus wall. If you have more than one room, you can use different paint colors. If your room is smaller, avoid using dark colors. Dark colors make your room feel gloomy.

1. _____

    There are various decorating styles. You can pick one, depending on your personal tastes. If you like antique style, consider decorating your house in a country French style. If you like clean lines and bold patterns, you should consider a contemporary look. There are also other decorating styles that you can take into consideration, including Southwestern, shabby chic, country, rococo, neoclassical, African, Asian, Mediterranean, and Victorian.

2. _____

    Color is also crucial in interior decoration. From furniture to decorations, if the color is off, the entire look will be poor. Certain themes need specific colors. Color schemes include navy blue, white, gold and cherry red. These colors work well for a nautical theme. Colors like ivory, white and yellow work well for a country French look. Colors, such as sage green, rose pink and white, go well for shabby chic. Black, white and dark blue go well for contemporary style, while gold, emerald green, and amber make your room warm.

3. _____

    Your space will look messy if you have poor organization. In order to make your room look more organized, you may specify certain areas for things that can be thrown around. For example, if you put your keys or mail on the table, prepare a decorative bowl on the table to hold these items. Under this circumstance, they are not just laying around in plain site. If you leave your magazines on the coffee table, put them in a drawer with hidden storage so that you can easily keep your magazines.

Unit

Technology

Warm up

A. Do you know "the development of technology"? Share what you know with your partner.

💡閱讀策略——閱讀掃描技巧複習

閱讀策略——閱讀掃描技巧複習

快速掃描下面的文章，這篇文章談論到哪些年代呢？將你的答案寫在下列空格中。

_____   _____

_____   _____

Reading

The Development of Technology

Since the Industrial Revolution in the 18th century, the development of technology has been fast and unpredictable. During this time, the steam engine was invented, and coal was used as the main source of energy. The steam engine helped develop textile manufacturing, mining, and transport. In the 19th century, transportation, construction, and communication technologies were further advanced. The steam engine continued to be used for both steamboat and railway transportation. Telegraphy was also developed to help communication. Moving on to the 20th century, the technology development in this age was a turning point for modern science and technology. New communication technology, transportation, and increased research all played important roles. First, radio, radar and early sound recording were created and developed into the telephone and fax machine. Second, energy and engine technology were greatly improved. Next, nuclear power was also discovered. Moreover, people began using computers, and scientists discovered DNA. In the 21st century, technology has leaped even further, especially in electronics and biotechnology. Internet access has also become part of people's everyday life in most countries. However, this is yet the end of technology development. Research continues into computers, nanotechnology, green technologies, and more efficient LEDs. What do you expect to see in the 22nd century?

💡閱讀策略——寫大意幫助理解

　　想要清楚地理解文章的架構和重點，你可以將一篇文章濃縮成大意（summary），也就是文章的重點內容。例如將上列文章每一個時期的科技發展用一個句子來描述。如此一來，便可更清楚地了解每一個時期的重點和整個文章的架構。

A. Read the article "The Development of Technology". Summarize each period with one sentence.

18th century: _____

_____

19th century: _____

_____

20th century: _____

_____

21st century: _____

_____

Vocabulary

A. Do you know the meanings of these words? Check them with your partner. Write the meanings next to the words.

1. industrial
2. development
3. unpredictable
4. steam
5. invent
6. manufacture
7. advance
8. increase
9. improve
10. nuclear

11. leap

12. electronic

13. access

💡單字策略——利用 word family 來幫助記憶及增加單字量

例如：

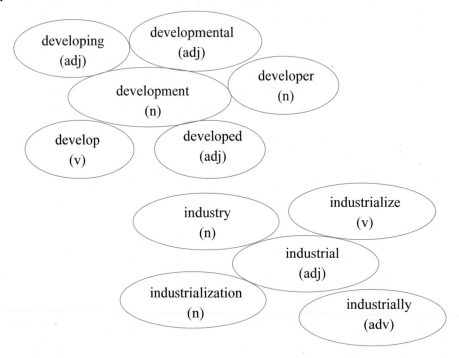

試試看將其它單字與它們的 word family 做連結。

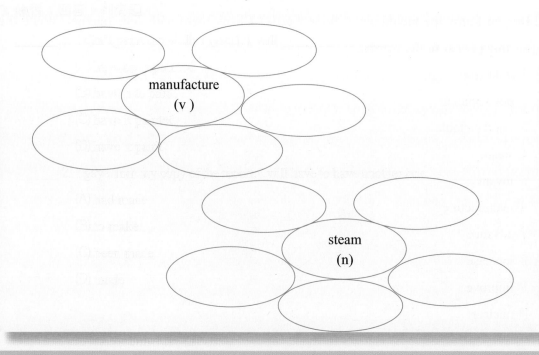

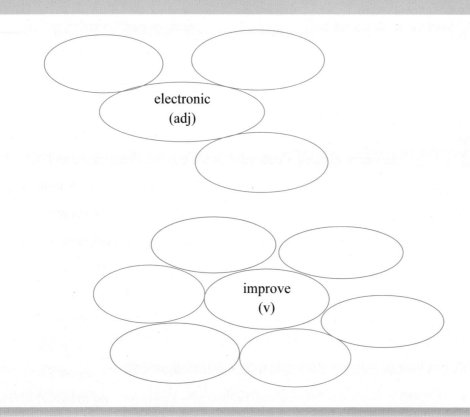

單字表

1. industrial [ɪnˈdʌstrɪəl]	(adj)工業的	例 The industrial revolution has changed the way people live.
2. development [dɪˈvɛləpmənt]	(n)生長；進化；發展	例 The development of technology is fast.
3. unpredictable [ʌnprɪˈdɪktəbl̩]	(adj)不可預料的	例 Whether he will come tomorrow is unpredictable.
4. steam [stim]	(n)蒸汽	例 Many people remember the steam trains in the old time.
5. invent [ɪnˈvɛnt]	(v)發明、創造	例 Elisha Otis invented the first safety brake for elevators.
6. manufacture [mænjəˈfæktʃɚ]	(v)製造, 加工	例 This company manufactures bikes.
7. advance [ədˈvæns]	(v)使向前移動；推進，促進	例 Wireless technology has been greatly advanced.
8. increase [ɪnˈkris]	(v)增加；增強	例 Machines have increased production.

9. improve [ɪmˈpruv]	(v)改進、改善；增進	例 My English is improved at the end of the course.
10. nuclear [ˈnjuklɪɚ]	(adj)原子核的；原子能的	例 Nuclear power may be cheap but can be dangerous.
11. leap [lip]	(v)跳、跳躍	例 The boy leaped across the fence.
12. electronic [ɪlɛkˈtrɑnɪk]	(adj)電子的	例 Electronic devices should be turned off while the plane takes off.
13. access [ˈæksɛs]	(n)進入；存取	例 Internet access is becoming easier and more convenient.

Grammar

A. 以下為不規則動詞三態表，請在空格中填入正確的動詞型態。

Present	Past	Past Participle
break	broke	
	brought	brought
buy	bought	
choose		chosen
drink	drank	
fall		fallen
freeze	froze	
	grew	grown
hide		hidden
lead	led	
lie		lain
ride		ridden
run	ran	
see	saw	
shake	shook	
	shone	shone
	shot	shot
steal		stole
wake	woke	
wear		worn

B. 閱讀下列例句，什麼時候使用過去簡單式（**past simple**）？什麼時候使用現在完成式（**present perfect**）？你知道它們的文法規則嗎？

1. Since the Industrial Revolution, the development of technology has been fast and unpredictable.

2. The 20th century technology was a turning point for modern science and technology.

3. In the 21st century, technology has leaped even further, especially in electronics and biotechnology.

4. Internet access has become part of people's everyday life in most countries.

5. I bought an iPhone yesterday. I have used it to call many of my friends.

6. John started learning English three years ago. He has learned English for three years.

C. 下列敘述哪一個是 **past simple** 的用法？哪一個是 **present perfect** 的用法？將這些敘述填入正確的空格中。

1. situations or actions that began in the past and still continue

2. completed actions in the past

3. focusing on the present result of a past action or recent event

4. referring to situations or actions in a time period up to now

Past simple	
Present perfect	

D. 選擇正確的答案：

Alice _____1._____ to New Zealand ten year ago. She _____2._____ there happily since then. Because Alice _____3._____ some Chinese courses when she was at university, she is able to teach some basic Chinese lessons there. She _____4._____ her husband at school. They _____5._____ married for more than five years. Jack is their only child.

_____ 1. (A) has moved   (B) moved   (C) moves

_____ 2. (A) has lived   (B) lived   (C) lives

_____ 3. (A) takes   (B) took   (C) has taken

_____ 4. (A) met   (B) has met   (C) meets

_____ 5. (A) got   (B) have got   (C) get

Speaking

A. Work in pairs. Talk about (1) when these items were invented, and (2) how they have influenced our daily life.

For example:

A: When was *an elevator* invented?

B: It was invented in 1852.

A: Who invented it?

B: The American inventor, Elisha Otis invented the first safety brake for elevators.

A: How has it influenced our daily life?

B: It has made going up and down a building more easily.

1852   elevator

1927   television

1876   telephone

1976   first personal computer

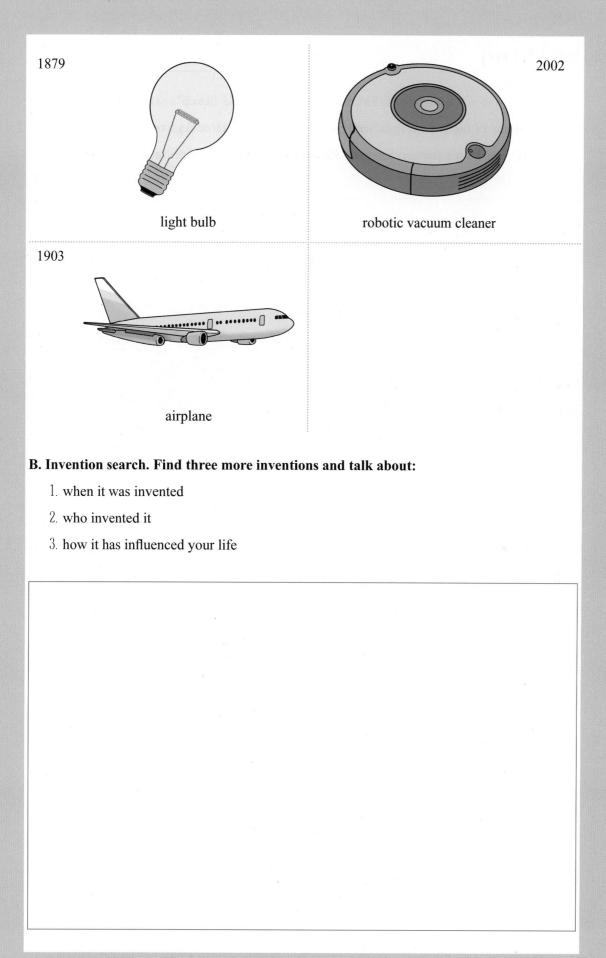

1879

light bulb

2002

robotic vacuum cleaner

1903

airplane

B. Invention search. Find three more inventions and talk about:

1. when it was invented
2. who invented it
3. how it has influenced your life

Writing

A. Write about an invention that has made your life much easier / comfortable / convenient. What is it? When did you start using it? How has your life become after using it? Start your paragraph with "Since I had a/an ..., my life has become ..."

_____

_____

_____

_____

_____

_____

_____

_____

B. How much do you still remember about your teens? How does your teenage life affect you? Write about what you did when you were younger and what you have become now. Start your paragraph with "Since ..., I have become more .... I remember when I was ..."

_____

_____

_____

_____

_____

_____

_____

_____

Listening

💡聽力策略──聽指引或是表達順序的字詞

　　要了解演講或談話，除了聽出關鍵字以外，另一個重點就是根據指引的句子（signposting phrases）或是表達順序的字詞（sequencing phrases）來理解整個談話的內容及架構。下列是一些例子：

Signposting phrases:

To start, I want to...

So, that covers...

Now I'll move onto...

Coming now to my last point, ...

Sequencing phrases:

First, I'd like to start by ...

Secondly, I'll ...

Next, I want to discuss ...

Finally, I'm going to ...

🎵 **Track 27**

A. Listen to a talk about "facebook". Write down the signposting phrases or sequencing phrases that help you understand the structure of the talk.

Signposting phrases and sequencing phrases:

1. *first*

2.

3.

4.

🎵 **Track 28**

B. Listen again. This time, pay attention to the key words after each signposting phrases or sequencing phrases. Write down the key words. Then number the sequence of what you hear.

Key words:

1. *popular*

2.

3.

4.

the sequence of what you hear:

_____ Games on facebook

_____ Updates on facebook

____1____ Popularity of facebook

_____ Photos on facebook

ESP

MY phone 5 specification:

Color

White or black

Cellular and wireless

UMTS/HSDPA/HSUPA (850, 900, 1900, 2100 MHz)

GSM/EDGE (850, 900, 1800, 1900 MHz)

80 2.11b/g/n Wi-Fi (802.11n 2.4GHz only)

Bluetooth 2.1 + EDR wireless technology

Display

Retina display

3.5-inch (diagonal) widescreen Multi-Touch display

960-by-640-pixel resolution at 326 ppi

800:1 contrast ratio (typical)

500 cd/m2 max brightness (typical)

Fingerprint-resistant oleo phobic coating on front and back

Support for display of multiple languages and characters simultaneously

Size and weight

Height: 4.5 inches (115.2 mm)

Width: 2.31 inches (58.6 mm)

Depth: 0.37 inch (9.3 mm)

Weight: 4.8 ounces (137 grams)

Capacity

16GB or 32GB flash drive

Camera, photos, and video

Video recording, HD (720p) up to 30 frames per second with audio

5-megapixel still camera

VGA-quality photos and video at up to 30 frames per second with the front camera

Tap to focus video or still images

LED flash

Photo and video geo-tagging

A. The above information introduces the MY phone 5. Use the vocabulary you have just learned to introduce your cell phone.

For example:

    Today I'm going to talk about my cell phone. First, I'll talk about its size and weight. The height is 4.5 inches, and the width is 2.31 inches. It's very light. It weighs only 137 grams. Next, for the camera, it's a 5-megapixel still camera with a LED flash. Finally, I'm going to present its display. It has a 3.5-inch widescreen and 960-by-640-pixel resolution.

Unit **12**

Novel & Music

Warm up

A. Do you like to read stories? Do you know how to read a story?

Reading

💡閱讀策略──利用故事分析圖

　　當我們閱讀故事時想要清楚地了解整個故事的來龍去脈，就必須對故事的主角（main characters）、背景（setting）、問題（problem）、事件（story events）及結局（ending）做一個分析。我們可以利用story map來幫助我們更加了解故事。

A. Read the story "The Man and His Donkey". Complete the story map below.

The Man and His Donkey

　　Once upon a tim e, there lived an old man with his son in the countryside. They kept a donkey. One day, the old man and his son were going to the market with their donkey. They walked by the sides of the donkey. Not long after they walked for a while, a woman passed them and said, "You fools, what is a donkey for? Why don't you ride on it?" After hearing what the woman had said, the old man put his boy on the donkey and they went on their way to the market.

　　A few minutes later, they passed a group of men. One of them said, "Look at that lazy young boy. He let his father walk while he rides on the donkey." As a result, the old man had his boy get off, and got on the donkey himself. However, as they came to the town, a woman carrying her baby said to her husband,"How can that lazy old man make his poor little son walk alone?" The old man really did not know what to do. He stopped and thought. At last, he decided to ask his boy to get up and sit in front of him on the donkey.

　　When they were riding on the donkey towards the market, some people began to jeer and point to them. The man stopped and asked why they were jeering at them. A man said, "Aren't you ashamed of yourselves? That poor donkey is overloaded." The old man and his boy got off the donkey and tried to think what to do. They thought and they thought. Then they cut down a small tree trunk and tied the donkey's feet to it. They raised the donkey with the tree trunk on their shoulders. However, everyone who met them laughed at them. As they came to a bridge, the donkey kicked his feet and caused the boy to drop the tree trunk. The donkey fell into the river and was drowned. The old man sighed and said, "Please all, and you will please none."

Story map:

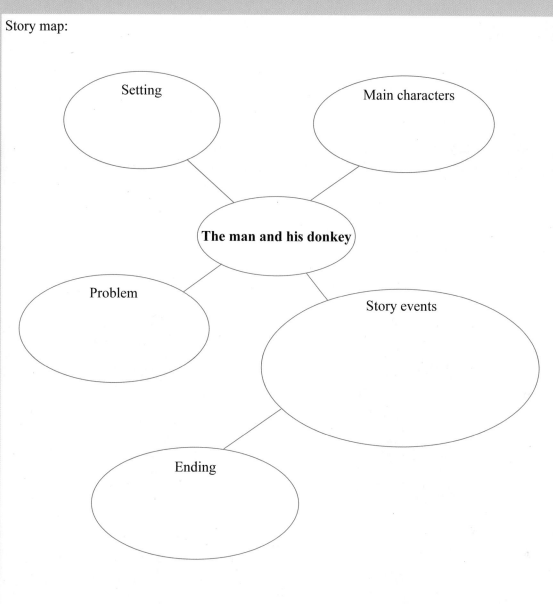

B. Do you still remember the story? Use the story map that you have just created and retell the story.

Vocabulary

圖像可以幫助你記憶單字的意義。現在就試著在下面的連環漫畫中指示出下列這些單字。（並非每個圖片皆有對應呈現的單字，一個圖片可能呈現多於一個單字。）

donkey	ride alone	jeer	point	ashamed	overload
tree trunk	tie	shoulder	kick	drown	sigh

1.
donkey

6.

2.

7.

3.

8.

4.

9.

5.

10.

單字表

1. donkey ['daŋkɪ]	(n)驢子	例 A donkey is smaller than a horse.
2. alone [ə'lon]	(adj)單獨的、獨自的 (adv)單獨地、獨自地	例 Nobody is at home. I am alone. 例 Coco works on her project alone.
3. jeer [dʒɪr]	(v)嘲笑、嘲弄	例 His friends did not jeer at his mistake but encouraged him to try again.
4. point ['pɔɪnt]	(v)指出、指向	例 She points to the sky and asks us to watch the rainbow.
5. ashamed [ə'ʃemd]	(adj)羞愧的、感到難為情的	例 He feels ashamed of lying to his parents.
6. overload ['ovɚ'lod]	(v)使超載、使負荷過多	例 The truck is overloaded.
7. trunk [trʌŋk]	(n)樹幹	例 The workers use trunks to build a bridge.
8. tie [taɪ]	(v)打結，繫上	例 The little child learns to tie her shoes.
9. shoulder ['ʃoldɚ]	(n)肩膀	例 Daniel puts his pet bird on his shoulder.
10. kick [kɪk]	(v)踢	例 He kicked the ball and scored a goal.
11. drown [draʊn]	(v)把…淹死	例 She fell into the river and was drowned.
12. sigh [saɪ]	(v)嘆氣，嘆息	例 The old man sighed for disappointment.

Grammar

A. 根據以下例句，將下列使役動詞（**causative verbs**）依照它們的用法歸類。

1. He let his father walk while he rides on the donkey.
2. The old man had his boy get off and got on the donkey himself.
3. How can that lazy old man make his poor little son walk alone?
4. The man got his boy to ride on the donkey.
5. She persuaded me to sign the contract.

6. John forced his employees to work overtime.

7. He ordered them to close the window.

8. Liz does not allow anyone to bother her when she's studying.

9. Few restaurants permit their customers to bring outside food.

10. Not every parent wants their children to make a lot of money.

Causative verbs:

| want | get | persuade | force | order |
| allow | permit | have | make | let |

1. 動詞 + 受詞 + to + 原形動詞	2. 動詞 + 受詞 + 原形動詞

 上列的 causative verbs 也有可能以「動詞 + 受詞 + 過去分詞」的型態出現

例如：They had all the computers repaired.

The boss wants the check cashed.

B. 練習：回答下列問題。

_____ 1. I can't paint the walls myself. I will _____.

　　(A) have been painted

　　(B) have it to paint

　　(C) have it painted

　　(D) have it paint

_____ 2. I gave Tom my copy of the report. I will have to have another one _____.

　　(A) had made

　　(B) to make

　　(C) been made

　　(D) made

_____ 3. The police officers ordered _____ put his hands on his head.

   (A) the robber

   (B) the robber to

   (C) to the robber

   (D) to be

_____ 4. These computers are too slow. Why don't you get someone _____

   them?

   (A) upgrade

   (B) to upgrade

   (C) upgrading

   (D) to be upgraded

_____ 5. My friends want _____ to a movie with them.

   (A) to go

   (B) me go

   (C) me to go

   (D) to me go

Speaking

A. Group discussion : Read the following problems. Suggest ways to solve the problems using causative verbs.

1. My backpack is too heavy.

   Solution: _You should get someone to help you._

2. Lisa's hair is too long.

   Solution: _____

3. My child is too dependent.

   Solution: _____

4. Rick's partners don't agree with him.

   Solution: _____

5. Zoe's computer is broken.

   Solution: _____

6. My foreign friends are coming to visit me.

   Solution: _____

7. Johnson doesn't like studying.

   Solution: _____

Writing

A. Make up a story or re-write a short story that you know. Use the story map to help you brainstorm ideas.

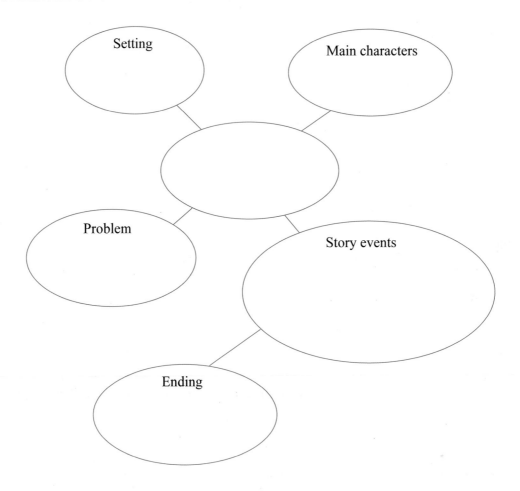

B. Write up your story.

Once upon a time, there lived _____

_____

_____

_____

_____

_____

_____

Listening

 Track 29

A. Listen to the song and complete the lyrics.

Are you lonesome tonight?   **By Al Jolson**

Are you lonesome tonight

Do you miss me tonight

Are you sorry we drifted _____1._____

Is the memory still _____2._____ your heart

Are you lonesome tonight

Do you miss me tonight

Are you sorry we drifted apart

Does your memory stray

To a bright summer day

When I kissed you and called you sweetheart

Do the _____3._____ in your parlor

Seem empty and bare

Do you gaze _____4._____ your doorstep and picture me there

Is your heart filled with pain

Shall I come _____5._____ again

Tell me dear, are you lonesome tonight

I wonder if you're lonesome tonight

You know someone said the world's a stage

And _____6._____ must play a part

Fate had me play a lover with you as my sweetheart

Act one was where we met

I loved you at first glance

You read your line so cleverly

And never _____7._____ a cue

Then came act two

And you seemed to change

You acted strange

Why? I'll never know

Then came the day

When you _____8._____ away and left me all alone

If you _____9._____ when you said you loved

I had no 'cause to doubt you

But I'd rather go on hearing your lies

Than go on living without you

The _____10._____ is bare and I'm standing there

In the part of a broken clown

And _____11._____ you won't come back to me

Then they can bring the curtain down

Is your heart _____12._____ with pain

Shall I come back again

Tell me dear, are you lonesome tonight

(Are you lonesome tonight)

💡聽力策略——注意結尾子音與連音

當我們在唱歌的時候，為了讓歌曲聽起來更流暢，連音就變得特別地重要。所以要聽懂英文歌曲很重要的一個關鍵，就是聽懂連音。而連音的關鍵通常在於結尾的子音與下一個字開頭的母音，例如在"Are you lonesome tonight?"這首歌曲中就有許多連音的地方，像 drifted apart, still in, kissed you, called you 等。

再聽一次這首歌，試著把其它連音找出來。

"Real" Languages in the Lord of the Rings

Many character and place names in The Lord of the Rings are related to words from old and modern languages. Hobbits, Elves, and Wizards are some examples of the historical links for some of Tolkien's characters and settings.

Some other examples:

Saruman's name	Anglo-Saxon, or Old English, "searu-" means cunning
Sauron	Icelandic stem meaning filth or uncleanness
Mordor	Old English "morthor" meaning murder
Middle-earth	The name for the Earth itself in Old English, meaning the battleground between the forces of good and evil.

On the other hand, the writer, John Tolkien invented languages for his characters and settings. "Quenya" is an example. This invented language was inspired by Finnish. Tolkien taught himself Finnish in order to read old Finnish songs and stories. In "The Lord of the Rings", invented languages play a very important role in the development of story. Examples of Tolkien's invented languages in "The Lord of the Rings" are as follows:

Invented language	Meaning in English
"Elen sila lumenn' omentielvo" (Quenya) "Ash nazg durbatuluk, ash nazg gimbatul, ash nazg thrakatuluk agh burzum-ishi krimpatul" (Black speech) "Khazad-ai-menu!" (Dwarvish)	A star shines on the hour of our meeting One Ring to rule them all, One Ring to find them, One Ring to bring them all and in the darkness bind them. The Dwarves are upon you!

A. Read the text above and answer the T / F questions.

_____ 1. Saruman's name has the meaning of cunning.

_____ 2. Murder in old English is "Morthor".

_____ 3. Tolkien's writing is influenced by French.

_____ 4. John Tolkien taught Finnish.

_____ 5. John Tolkien invented languages for his story.

Unit **13**

Life Health
Omega 3 Oil

Biology

Warm up

A. Do you know Jet Li, Elvis Presley, Leonardo Dicaprio and Jackie Chan? What kinds of personalities do you think they have? Discuss with your partners.

Jet Li

Elvis Presley

Leonardo Dicaprio

Jackie Chan

Reading

A. Read the article "Blood Types and Personalities." What types of blood do these people have?

Blood Types and Personalities

第1行   Do you know your friends' blood types? You may be able to guess the correct answers if you know their personalities well. The idea of blood type and personalities was introduced by Takeji Furukawa in 1927. He believed that personalities were related to blood types. Generally, people with type A blood would be <u>reserved</u> because they don't like to show their feelings or to tell people what

第5行   they think. They would also be <u>patient</u>. They can wait for a long time without getting angry. Moreover, type As are mostly good listeners but they could be <u>stubborn</u>. You will find it difficult to change their

144 Way to go

mind! Jet Li is one famous person who has type A blood. As for type B people, they can be <u>creative</u> and <u>passionate</u>.

第10行

They can always think of something new and are always interested in everything. Besides, type Bs would be <u>ambitious</u>. They always want to be successful, rich, and powerful. They would also be self-confident, too. However, they might be forgetful sometimes. Leonardo Dicaprio is a type B person.

People with type O blood are believed to be the most easygoing of all. Type Os love to make friends though they can be <u>insensitive</u>. They don't easily get how other people feel and are likely to hurt people.

第15行

Elvis Presley is one of the famous people with type O blood. Finally, type AB is a special case. People who have type AB blood would be cool and <u>rational</u>. They listen for reasons. The negative side of type ABs might be their indecisiveness. Can you believe that Jackie Chan is one of the type ABs?

Do you know what your best friend's blood type is? Guess it now!

閱讀策略—— 依上下文猜字的意思

當我們在閱讀的時候常常會遇到一些我們不懂的單字或是具有不只一個意義的單字，我們可以透過上下文來猜測這些單字的意思。例如：當我們看到文章內容描述 Type A, B, O 及 AB 我們不免聯想到血型，因此我們可以推測 blood types 詞中的 blood 就是「血」的意思。又例如我們可以從第四行 "reserved" 這個字接下來的句子 "they don't like to show their feelings or to tell people what they think" 推測 "reserved" 應該有「不愛表達的」、「含蓄的」的意思。

現在就試著透過上下文推測其它字的意思。你認為下列單字是什麼意思呢？你如何從上下文推測出這些字的意思呢？把你的答案寫在下列的表格中。

單字	意思	上下文
patient (Line 5)		
stubborn (Line 6)		
creative (Line 7)		
passionate (Line 7)		
ambitious (Line 9)		
insensitive (Line 12)		
rational (Line 14)		

B. Which blood type does your friend have? Which blood type does your teacher have? Think about their personalities and guess about it.

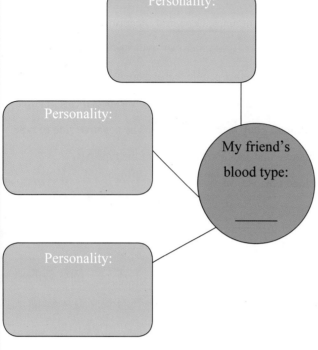

Personality:

Personality:

Personality:

My friend's blood type:

_____

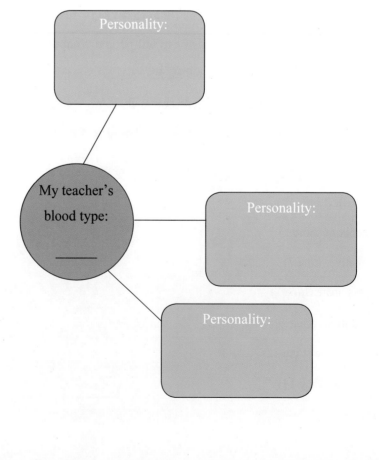

Personality:

My teacher's blood type:

_____

Personality:

Personality:

Vocabulary

A. **Do you understand these words? Which word is positive (+) and which word is negative (-)? Put the words in the correct box below.**

| reserved | patient | stubborn | creative | passionate | forgetful |
| ambitious | self-confident | insensitive | indecisive | rational | |

Positive	Negative

💡單字策略──字首記憶法

　　英文的字根及字首也可以幫助我們理解單字的意思。例如：字首 an-, in-, un-, dis- 及 non- 有 "not" 的意思，像 anemia（貧血），inconvenient（不方便的），unhappy（不快樂的），disappear（不見、消失）和 non-profit（非營利的）。

　　單字單元中的 insensitive 及 indecisive 就有「不」的意思。

　　另外其它單字也可以加上這些字首變成具有「不」意思的字。試試看把下列單字變成有「不」意思的相反詞。

1. reserved →

2. patient →

3. creative →

4. passionate →

5. forgetful →

6. ambitious →

7. rational →

B. **Use two of the words that you have just learned to describe yourself. Share with your classmate.**

A: I think I am _____ and/but _____.

B: Yes, you are. (No, you're not. You are _____ and/but _____.)

單字表

1. personality ['pɜsn'ælətɪ]	(n)人格、品格	例 We need to respect people of different personality types.
2. blood [blʌd]	(n)血液	例 I am afraid of seeing blood.
3. reserved [rɪ'zɜvd]	(adj)沈默寡言的；含蓄的	例 She doesn't talk a lot. She is very reserved.
4. patient ['peʃənt]	(adj)有耐心的、能容忍的	例 He never gets angry for waiting friends. He's so patient.
5. stubborn ['stʌbən]	(adj)倔強的、頑固的	例 Never think of changing his mind. He is very stubborn.
6. creative [krɪ'etɪv]	(adj)有創造力的	例 Michelle is such a creative person. She always has new ideas.
7. passionate ['pæʃənɪt]	(adj)熱情的	例 Peter is so passionate to every guest.
8. ambitious [æm'bɪʃəs]	(adj)有雄心的	例 Wayne is ambitious. He wants to be the best actor of the world.
9. insensitive [ɪn'sɛnsətɪv]	(adj)感覺遲鈍的	例 The candidate failed in this election because he was insensitive to people's lives.
10. rational ['ræʃənl]	(adj)理性的	例 You need to make a rational decision for your future.
11. indecisive ['ɪndɪ'saɪsɪv]	(adj)無決斷力的；優柔寡斷的	例 She always can't make up her mind. She is so indecisive.
12. forgetful [fə'gɛtfəl]	(adj)健忘的	例 I often forget where my keys are. I am so forgetful.

Grammar

A. 閱讀下列例句。哪一句呈現一個現在事實（**a present fact**）？哪一句是一個與現在事實相反的陳述（**an unreal present statement**）？

1. I am a reliable person. You can trust me.

2. If I were more reliable, you would trust me.

3. I wish I were more reliable.

B. 閱讀下列例句。試著找出與現在事實相反陳述的文法結構，把它寫在下面的空格中。

If Mary were taller, she would join the basketball team.

If it were raining, Tom would stay at home.

You wouldn't buy beef if you didn't eat it.

I wish I had a car so I could drive to school.

Carol wishes her friend bought her a gift.

句型結構：

1. If 主詞 + _____, 主詞 + _____.

   = 主詞 + _____ if 主詞 + _____.

2. I wish + 主詞 + _____.

C. 運用上述文法完成下列句子並與你的同學分享你的句子。

1. If I were _____, _____.

2. I wish _____.

Speaking

A. Work in groups. Take turns to make sentences using the "if" subjunctives. Which group can make more sentences?

Starting with:

If I were more ambitious, **I would be more successful**.

→**If I were more successful,** I would make a lot of money.

→If I made a lot of money, I would ...

Writing

A. Are you satisfied with your study, personalities, appearances, life, home or the like?

Choose a topic.

Write a short paragraph describing what you wish you would have or be like.

Use "I wish ..." and "if..." clauses.

For example:

I wish I were more sociable. My sister can make friends very easily and her friends like her. She always invites her friends over to her house. I am not like her. I often don't know how to get along with my friends. If I were more sociable, I would make more friends. I would have people to have fun with and I would not be all by myself most of the time.

_____
_____
_____
_____
_____
_____
_____

Listening

Read the information about blood types and personalities below.

Blood Type	Personalities
A	reserved, patient, stubborn
B	creative, passionate, forgetful
O	ambitious, self-confident, insensitive
AB	cool, rational, indecisive

Track 30

A. Listen to a conversation. Guess which blood type Lily has according to the chart.

Lily   Blood type _____

當我們聽英文的時候，不一定會直接聽到答案，而是要透過關鍵字來猜測正確答案。例如：聽剛才的對話時，我們會聽到 ambitious, self-confident 和 insensitive。透過這三個關鍵字我們可以去推測 Lily 的血型是 O 型。

　　現在就用這個方法試著做下面的練習。

Track 31

B. Listen to three more conversations. Guess which blood type Johnson, Ruth and Rod have. Write the correct answer next to each picture.

Johnson

Blood type _____

Ruth

Blood type _____

Rod

Blood type _____

It is very important for people especially nurses and pharmacists to know about the ingredients, directions, and effects of medicines and health food. The following is an example of "Omega 3 Oil".

A. Fill in the blanks with the words below.

direction	ingredient	capsules	warning	description

Product: Life Health Omega 3 Oil

Price: US$: 30.00

Product size: 180 1._____

2._____ : Take one capsule with meals, 3 times a day.

3._____ :

Life Health Omega 3 Oil contains 70% salmon oil. Omega 3 oil is necessary for our body health. The Omega-3 triglycerides EPA and DHA can be taken as a dietary supplement. The omega-3 triglycerides have an anti-inflammatory activity in the body. Omega 3 oil is also beneficial for supporting and maintaining healthy retina and eye function

4._____ :

Each capsule contains 1000mg of deep sea fish oil.

5._____ :

Consult your doctor before use.

Store in a cool, dry place.

Do not use if the seal is broken.

Unit

14

Fashion Design

Warm up

A. Do you know anyone who has never given up pursuing his/her dream? Write down your answers in the box below.

B. Skim the article. How much do you know about Johan Ku?

Predict from the pictures.

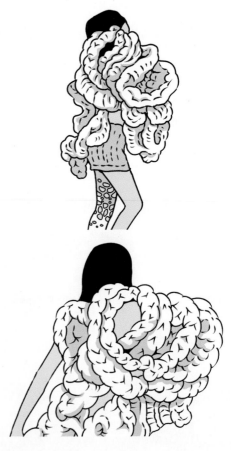

Reading

💡閱讀策略——瀏覽閱讀法

跳過不懂的單字，快速地瀏覽下面的文章，你可以了解多少關於設計師古又文（Johan Ku）的報導呢？一分鐘時間開始倒數計時。

Johan Ku, Another "Glory of Taiwan"

Johan Ku, a Taiwanese fashion designer, won the Avant-Garde Prize in Gen Art Style 2009 in New York with his knitwear sculpture. He has proven that hard work can make dreams come true. Johan is not from a rich family. He was born in Taipei in 1979 and raised by his mother who worked as a street cleaner. "If I hadn't got support from my mom, I wouldn't have pursued my dream", said Johan. Ku's mother never stopped Johan from pursuing what he really liked, such as watching Taiwanese opera and Japanese cartoons in his childhood. Johan loved comic books most. To him, reading them was like watching movies on paper.

At an early age, Johan wanted to become a comic artist. He chose to study advertising design in high school and began working as a freelance graphic designer at the age of 17. After graduation, he entered university and majored in fashion and textile design. After one year of study in the university, Johan thought of transferring to another school. However, reading Coco Chanel's biography made him decide to be a fashion designer rather than a graphic designer. He did part-time designing jobs, obtained scholarships, and got student loans. Johan got both his bachelor and master degrees in fashion and textile design. However, Johan thought it was not enough. He started to save money for overseas studies. His hard-working and nonstop pursuit of his dream had made "another glory of Taiwan."

In March 2010, Johan held his exhibition at the Taipei Fine Art Museum with his award-winning collections. His creations have been defined as a new form of fine art. Johan offered some advice for new Taiwanese designers - "If I had given up my dream, I wouldn't have been a fashion designer. As long as you dream big and never give up, you can make it."

A. Read again. Answer the following true or false questions.

_____ 1. Johan was born into a rich family.

_____ 2. Johan's mother wanted him to study fashion design.

_____ 3. Johan majored in graphic design at university.

_____ 4. Coco Chanel's story made Johan want to become a fashion designer.

_____ 5. Johan saved money to study abroad.

_____ 6. Johan gave up his dream once before.

Vocabulary

💡單字策略——造句法

　　當我們把所學的單字造句，記憶就不容易消退，所以為學到的單字造句能夠幫助我們牢牢記住這個單字的意義及用法。

A. Group work：Find out the meanings and usage of the words. Then make a sentence for each word.

1. knitwear: _____

2. sculpture: _____

3. pursue: _____

4. freelance: _____

5. graphic designer: _____

6. textile: _____

7. transfer: _____

8. obtain: _____

9. scholarship: _____

10. loan: _____

11. bachelor: _____

12. master: _____

13. overseas: _____

單字表

1. knitwear [ˈnɪtˌwɛr]	(n)針織衣物	例 The designer won the award with his knitwear collection.
2. sculpture [ˈskʌlptʃɚ]	(n)雕刻品、雕塑品	例 Many sculptures are displayed in the museum.

3. pursue [pɚˈsu]	(v)追求	例 He never gives up pursuing his dream.
4. freelance [ˈfriˈlɑns]	(adj)自由作家（或演員等）的；獨立的	例 She works as a freelance designer.
5. graphic [ˈgræfɪk]	(adj)繪畫的	例 John studied graphic design at college.
6. textile [ˈtɛkstaɪl]	(n)紡織品；紡織原料 (adj)紡織的	例 The textile industry has grown since the 80s.
7. transfer [trænsˈfɚ]	(v)改變、轉變；轉校、轉科	例 I transferred to a public school last year.
8. obtain [əbˈten]	(v)得到、獲得	例 He has obtained many prizes.
9. scholarship [ˈskɑlɚˌʃɪp]	(n)獎學金	例 Lisa obtains a scholarship to study in New Zealand.
10. loan [lon]	(n)貸款	例 She will apply for student loans to pay for the tuition.
11. bachelor [ˈbætʃələ]	(n)學士	例 I obtained my Bachelor degree three years ago.
12. master [ˈmæstɚ]	(n)碩士	例 A number of people in Taiwan have a Maser degree.
13. overseas [ˌovɚˈsiz]	(adj)在海外的 (adv)在海外地	例 This product is sold to overseas markets. 例 Mary is studying overseas.

Grammar

A. 下列句子具有與過去事實相反的意思，請找出它的文法規則。

1. If I hadn't got support from my mom, I wouldn't have pursued my dream.

2. If I had given up my dream, I wouldn't have been a fashion designer.

3. I wouldn't have changed my mind if I hadn't read Coco Chanel's bibliography.

4. I wouldn't have been a fashion designer if I had chosen to be a graphic designer.

句型結構：

If 主詞 + _____ , 主詞 + _____

= 主詞 + _____ if 主詞 + _____ .

B. Practice: Choose the best response.

_____ 1. If Tom _____ harder, he wouldn't have failed the exam last week.

(A) has studied

(B) studied

(C) had studied

(D) did not study

_____ 2. If my friend _____ me, I would have forgotten our meeting.

(A) did not remind

(B) was not reminded

(C) does not remind

(D) had not reminded

_____ 3. If you _____ any question, you can call this number at anytime.

(A) had had

(B) have

(C) had

(D) has had

_____ 4. We _____ to Japan if the typhoon had not swept our hometown last week.

(A) would have travelled.

(B) had travelled.

(C) have travelled.

(D) would travelled

Speaking

A. Role-play: Choose one of the situations. Practice with your partner. Use as many unreal past "if-clauses" as possible.

<u>Scenario 1:</u> You and your partner are talking about your last trip. It was fun but could be much better. Talk about what you could do but you didn't or what you shouldn't have done but you did.

> *For example–*
>
> *A: Do you still remember our last trip to Taipei?*
>
> *B: Yeah! It was fun but it could have been much better.*
>
> *A: I agree. If we had booked a better hotel, we would have had a more comfortable room.*
>
> *B: And if we had traveled by train, we wouldn't have wasted so much time.*

<u>Scenario 2:</u> You and your partner are talking about your last English exam. You think you could do much better.

<u>Scenario 3:</u> You and your partner are talking about the last decision you made. You think other choices may be better for you.

Writing

A. Brainstorming: Search for a person who has had a great achievement. Find out what he/she had done at the early age in order to make him/herself successful now. Use the outlining technique you have learned in Unit 1 to outline the information below.

B. Use the outline you've made to write a composition. (Use at least 3 unreal past "if-clauses".)

_____ (*Name of the person*) *is a renowned* _____

_____

_____

_____

_____

_____

_____

Listening

💡聽力策略——聽 wh- 字眼

　　想要更了解訪問的內容，聽懂訪問者的問題是很重要的，而想要聽懂問題就必須注意問題中的關鍵字，也就是 where, what, why, how, who, when 等，以及句子的主要動詞。

Track 32

A. Listen to the interview with another famous fashion designer, Cecilia Lee. "What are the interview questions?" Check the questions that you hear.

☐ Where are you from?

☐ Where do you live now?

☐ Who supported you to become a designer?

☐ How did you pursue your dream?

☐ What inspired you to become a fashion designer?

☐ What are your must-have items?

☐ What's your personal style?

☐ What are you wearing right now?

☐ When's your first exhibit?

Track 33

B. Listen again. Answer the questions that you've checked.

ESP

A. Match the hairstyle with the correct picture.

1. shag

2. pigtail

3. bob

4. bun

5. pony tail

6. crew cut

7. Beatle cut

8. long waved hair

9. long straight hair

10. bangs

a.

b.

c.

d.

e.

f.

g.

h.

i.

j.

B. Maggie just got up! She is going an important meeting. Help her number the steps for putting on her make-up.

_____ put on some face cream

__1__ wash her face

_____ put some blusher on her cheeks

_____ put on some lotion

_____ use a powder puff to put on some powder

_____ put on some make-up base

_____ use a make-up sponge to put on foundation

_____ put on some lipstick

_____ put on some eye shadow

Unit **15**

Sport

Warm Up

A. Look at the following photos. Match the sport with its name

soccer

baseball

tennis

basketball

Reading

Statistics of Sports Injury

第1行   In the United States, about 30 million children and teenagers take part in some sports. Almost one-third of all injuries in childhood are sports-related injuries. Among these injuries, the most common ones are sprains and strains. Sprains refer to injuries that are caused by being stretched beyond their normal capacity, while strains are muscle tears caused in the same 第5行 manner. Actually, some sports are more dangerous than others. For example, a contact sport means players may touch each other, such as football or soccer. Such sport can be expected to result in more injuries than a non-contact sport which is a sport without physical contact such as swimming. According to the report made from National SAFE KIDS Campaign and the American Academy of Pediatrics, the statistics of the injury rates are shown as follows:

第10行 **Types of sports and the injury rates:**

Basketball is a team sport. It is played in two teams of five players who try to score points against one another by placing a ball through a 10-foot high hoop; that is, the goal for the players. Basketball is one of the most popular sports in the world. However, more than 207,000 children aged five to 14 were treated in hospital emergency

rooms for basketball-related injuries.

Baseball is a bat-and-ball sport played between two teams of nine players each. The goal is to score runs by hitting a thrown ball with a bat and touching a series of four bases at the corners of a square or diamond. Players in one team take turns hitting against the 第20行 pitcher of the other team. The <u>pitcher</u> is, by definition, the player who needs to throw a ball to the hitter who needs to hit the ball with a bat. Both teams try to stop the other from scoring runs by getting hitters out in several ways. Nevertheless, nearly 117,000 children aged five to 14 were treated in hospital emergency rooms for baseball-related injuries. Baseball also has the highest fatality rate among sports for children aged five to 14, with three to four children dying from baseball injuries each year.

第25行 **Soccer** is a team sport played between two teams of eleven players using a spherical ball. The object of the game is to score by driving the ball into the opposing goal. In a general play, the <u>goalkeepers</u> are the only players allowed to use their hands or arms to propel the ball; the rest of the team usually use their feet to kick the ball into position. It is considered to be the most popular sport in the world. The game is played on a 第30行 rectangular grass. Yet, about 76,000 children aged five to 14 were treated in hospital emergency rooms for soccer-related injuries.

A. Read the article above and answer the questions.

_____ 1. What does the word "sprain" in line 3 refer to?

(A) A kind of injury caused by stretching.

(B) A kind of injury caused by muscular tears.

(C) A kind of injury caused by physical contact.

(D) A kind of injury caused by muscular aches.

_____ 2. What does the word "strain" in line 4 refer to?

(A) A kind of injury caused by stretching.

(B) A kind of injury caused by muscular tears.

(C) A kind of injury caused by physical contact.

(D) A kind of injury caused by muscular aches.

_____ 3. What does the word "contact sport" in line 5 refer to?

(A) A sport that avoids physical contact.

(B) A sport that has physical contact.

(C) A sport that results in less injuries.

(D) A sport that is played by 3.5 million children a year.

Unit 15 ➡ Sport 165

_____ 4. What does the word "pitcher" in line 19 mean?

   (A) A player who needs to catch the ball.

   (B) A player who needs to throw the ball.

   (C) A player who needs to hit the ball.

   (D) A player who needs to propel the ball.

_____ 5. What does the word "goalkeeper" in line 28 mean?

   (A) A player who can catch the ball.

   (B) A player who can throw the ball.

   (C) A player who can hit the ball with a bat.

   (D) A player who can propel the ball with hands.

閱讀策略——文章掃瞄技巧

當你看文章的時候，要如何快速地找到重點呢？文章的重點大多是 who, where, what, when, why, and how，所以在看文章的時候你必須很快的看過每個句子，然後找出這幾個重點，「是什麼人、在哪裡、什麼時候、做了什麼事情、為什麼、如何做這件事情」，除此之外，數字、斜體字等也是重點，現在就趕快看看文章有沒有這些重點吧。

B. Read the article again and answer the following questions

_____ 1. According to the article, how many children or teenagers get injured in sports?

   (A) About 30 million

   (B) About 3.5 million

   (C) About 10 million

   (D) About 3 million

_____ 2. According to the article, what kind of sport is more dangerous than others?

   (A) Noncontact sport

   (B) Contact sport

   (C) Swimming

   (D) Aerobics

_____ 3. According to the article, how many children aged five to 14 got injured when playing basketball?

    (A) About 207,000 children

    (B) About 117, 000 children

    (C) About 30,000 children

    (D) About 76,000 children

_____ 4. According to the article, where can we play baseball?

    (A) In a court

    (B) On a diamond field

    (C) On a rectangular field

    (D) In a town square

_____ 5. According to the article, who is the only player allowed to use their hands when playing soccer?

    (A) A pitcher

    (B) A catcher

    (C) A goalkeeper

    (D) A hitter

Vocabulary

💡單字策略——單字分類法

    用分類法背單字的時候可以先將單字依照屬性分類，例如：可以依照功能、特性、詞性來等分類。例如：sprain 跟 strain 都屬於 injury 類。

單字表

1. injury ['ɪndʒərɪ]	(n)傷害	例 Teachers in the daycare center need to protect the children from injuries.
2. statistics [stə'tɪstɪks]	(n)統計	例 The statistics showed that many people die from cancers.
3. sprain [spren]	(n) (v)扭傷	例 He fell and sprained his ankle.
4. strain [stren]	(n) (v)拉傷	例 Carelessness will cause muscle strain during sports.

5. stretch [strɛtʃ]	(n) (v)伸展	例 You need to have a stretch before you start to swim.
6. capacity [kə`pæsətɪ]	(n)能力	例 My sister has a great capacity for learning many skills at one time.
7. tear [tɛr]	(v)撕裂；拉扯	例 The dog tore the newspaper into pieces.
8. contact [`kɑntækt]	(v) (n)接觸	例 I still keep in contact with some of my high school classmates.
9. pediatrics [ˌpidɪ`ætrɪks]	(n)小兒科	例 If the patients are over 21 years old, they are not supposed to go to the pediatrics when they are sick.
10. hoop [hup]	(n)鐵環；籃框	例 If you throw the ball into that hoop, you will gain two points for your team.
11. emergency [ɪ`mɝdʒənsɪ]	(n)緊急情況	例 When we go to a public place, we usually need to pay attention to the emergency doors.
12. pitcher [`pɪtʃɚ]	(n)投手	例 Mr. Wang is the best pitcher that I have ever known.
13. hitter [`hɪtɚ]	(n)打擊手	例 He has been named the greatest hitter in this game.
14. fatality [fə`tælətɪ]	(n)致命	例 That train accident caused many fatalities.
15. spherical [`sfɛrəkl̩]	(adj)球型的	例 Lanterns are usually made in a spherical shape.
16. opposing [ə`pozɪŋ]	(adj)相對的	例 Soccer players need to kick the ball into the opposing goal.
17. propel [prə`pɛl]	(v)推動	例 The engine propels the ship.
18. rectangular [rɛk`tæŋgjələ-]	(adj)長方形的	例 The desks in our classroom are rectangular.

現在來練習一下，將下面的單字做分類，看看它們是屬於形狀、人還是傷害的類別：

1. pitcher, hitter 屬於＿＿＿＿＿

2. spherical, rectangular 屬於＿＿＿＿＿

3. injury, tear, emergency, fatality 屬於＿＿＿＿＿

Grammar

Infinitive（不定詞）用來表達目的或是回答「為什麼」。

1. Such sport can be <u>expected to result</u> in more injuries than a non-contact sport which is a sport without physical contact such as swimming.

2. Basketball is a team sport. Such sports should be played in two teams of five players who <u>try to score</u> points against one another by placing a ball through a 10 foot high hoop.

3. The goal <u>is to score</u> runs by hitting a thrown ball with a bat and touching a series of four bases at the corners of a square or diamond.

4. The object of the game <u>is to score</u> by driving the ball into the opposing goal.

5. It is <u>considered to be</u> the most popular sport in the world.

綜合以上的句子，可以歸納出下列句型：

1. S + can + be + pp

2. S + try

3. S + be ＿＿＿＿ + ＿＿＿ to ＿＿＿ + ＿＿＿＿＿＿

4. It is ...

常與不定詞連用的動詞有：

hope	plan	intend	decide	promise	seem	appear
ask	want	need	agree	offer	pretend	

A. Choose the correct answer for the following sentences.

＿＿＿＿ 1. He did not have any money, so he decided ＿＿＿＿＿＿ a job

    (A) find   (B) finding   (C) to find   (D) found

＿＿＿＿ 2. I have prepared for this exam for such a long time so I expect ＿＿＿＿＿＿ it.

    (A) to pass   (B) past   (C) passed   (D) pass

_____ 3. The teacher seems _____ in a good mood.

    (A) was   (B) be   (C) to be   (D) been

_____ 4. I am so tired, so I need _____ a break.

    (A) taken   (B) took   (C) take   (D) to take

_____ 5. Did Carol agree _____ camping with you?

    (A) to go   (B) went   (C) gone   (D) go

Writing

A. Describe your favorite sport and explain how to play it and why it is your favorite one. State the main idea of each paragraph in its first sentence.

Paragraph 1. My favorite sport is ...

Paragraph 2. ... is a kind of sport which ...

Paragraph 3. ... is my favorite sport because ...

B. List three details that explain the main idea of each paragraph shown above.

Paragraph 1

    Detail 1: _____

    Detail 2: _____

    Detail 3: _____

Paragraph 2

    Detail 1: _____

    Detail 2: _____

    Detail 3: _____

Paragraph 3

    Detail 1: _____

    Detail 2: _____

    Detail 3: _____

C. Compose all your ideas by using the outline above. You may use the following sentence patterns.

Sentence Patterns

Definition	Reason
◆ ..., by definition, is ...	◆ I like ... because
◆ ... means ...	◆ I am fond of ... since
◆ ... is a kind of sport that ...	◆ ... is my favorite sport for that ...
	◆ Due to ... , I like ...
	◆ Owing to ... , I love...

_____

_____

_____

_____

_____

_____

_____

Speaking

A. Introduce a sport that you want to learn more about or you are already good at playing. Use search engines like Yahoo, Google, or Wikipedia to find the information you need for the speech.

Sport you want to learn/sport you are good at playing:
Where do people play this sport?
What equipment do people use to play this sport?
What are the rules of this sport?
Other information about this sport:

如何善用開頭語及結尾語

當你以英語演說的時候，通常需要一個開頭語先介紹演說內容的大概，這樣可以吸引聽眾的注意力。當你演說結束時，也需要使用結尾句來讓聽眾知道你的演說結束。

B. Use the information you have found. Show and tell how to play this sport.

Sentence patterns:

Sentences to start your speech	Sentences to end up your speech
Today I would like to introduce ...	This is the end of my speech.
The sport I am going to introduce is ...	That's about all of my speech
Do you know how to play ...? Let me ...	Thanks for listening.
Playing ... is very ...	Thanks for your attention.
... is a kind of sport that ...	If you have further questions, please feel free to ask.

Listening

聽力策略——擷取重點

試著把注意力放在某些關鍵字詞上面。做聽力測驗時，通常聽力測驗題目一開始會有 wh- 問句，藉由問句開頭字詞可以大概知道你需要注意的重點在哪裡。例如：如果是有關於 what 就必須將重點著重於找出事物；如果是有關於 who 就必須找出人物；如果是 when 就必須找出時間；如果是 where 就必須找出地點；如果是 how many 及 how much 就必須找出數字。

以下為聽力內容參考單字：

1. breaststroke [`brɛst,strok] (n) 蛙式	3. recovery [rɪ`kʌvərɪ] (n) 恢復，復甦；復原，痊癒
2. bend [bɛnd] (v) 使彎曲，折彎	4. freestyle [`fri,staɪl] (n)（游泳等）自由式

5. snap [snæp] (v) 使發劈啪聲；捻（手指）使劈啪作聲；啪地關上（或打開等）	10. float [flot] (v) 漂浮，浮動；飄動
6. glide [glaɪd] (v) 滑動，滑行	11. stroke [strok] (n) 游泳的一划；划法
7. sweep [swip] (v) 連綿，延伸	12. twist [twɪst] (v) 扭轉；扭彎；旋轉
8. outward [`autwɚd] (adv) 向外	13. breathe [brið] (v) 呼吸；呼氣；吸氣
9. inward [`ɪnwɚd] (adv) 向內；向中心	14. cheek [tʃik] (n) 臉頰

Track 34

A. Listen to the statements and choose the best answer.

_____ 1. What sport is the speaker going to teach?

    (A) swimming   (B) surfing   (C) skiing   (D) diving

_____ 2. How many steps does the breaststroke consist of?

    (A) Two   (B) Three   (C) Four   (D) Five

_____ 3. How much time should we glide?

    (A) two minutes   (B) two seconds

    (C) twelve minutes   (D) twelve seconds

_____ 4. How many phases does the pull include?

    (A) Two   (B) Three   (C) Four   (D) Five

Track 35

B. Listen to the statements and choose the best answer.

_____ 1. What is the passage mainly about?

    (A) surfing   (B) swimming   (C) snorkeling   (D) diving

_____ 2. How often should we take a breath while learning this kind of style?

    (A) every stroke   (B) every two strokes

    (C) every three strokes   (D) every four strokes

_____ 3. How many steps a learner needs to go through in learning this style?

    (A) two   (B) three   (C) four   (D) five

_____ 4. What is the last part of this style?

    (A) pull   (B) push   (C) kick   (D) catch

💡專業文章閱讀策略──尋找重點字以看懂運動專業文章

　　先看標題，從標題猜測文章可能會講什麼，之後看每段的第一句，可以幫助你猜測每一段的主旨大概在講什麼。接下來開始找每段的重點字，重點字不外乎「人」、「事」、「時」、「地」、「物」、「爲什麼」以及「如何」。下面的文章中，因爲標題著重於 how，所以在每段的重點中應該找尋如何防止運動傷害的方法，因此文章中的動詞及名詞等就可能是重點字。現在就讓我們用這個方法來讀下面這篇文章。

How to Avoid Injuries in Sports

Getting hurt is common when playing sports, especially after a certain age. Although certain injuries are unavoidable, we need to learn some strategies to prevent avoidable injuries. Some advice to reduce the risks is provided as follows:

Step 1

Stretch before and after sports training or games. Do not underestimate the importance of warming up or stretching before physical activities. Your body will have a wider range of motion when you gain such flexibility and this will increase its resistance to injuries.

Step 2

Focus. Most sports are highly competitive so we need to concentrate at all times. Any distractions should be ignored on the court or field. For example, if you are doing gymnastics, you should ignore sideline distractions. No matter what sport you practice, you should always stay focused.

Step 3

Strengthen the midsection. The abdominal and lower back muscles play an important role when playing sport games. It is common to have an injury if the muscles are not well trained. We pay much more attention to the abdomen; however, the lower back muscles are equally important.

Step 4

Develop your self confidence. You may suffer an injury if you feel you did not prepare well or if you are unsure whether you will perform well during the game. Even though you are not well-prepared for the big event, staying confident may help you perform better.

A. According to the text, the four ways to avoid sports injuries include:

1. _____

2. _____

3. _____

4. _____

Unit **16**

Education

Warm Up

A. Talk about your educational background.

B. Do you know the educational systems of other countries?

Reading

Educational Systems of Japan and the US

第1行　　America and Japan school structures differ in many styles of education. Although the common goal of each country is to teach necessary skills and knowledge to the next generation, the methods are distinct.

　　The most significant difference is the curriculum design between these two countries. 第5行 The Japanese Ministry of Education created a national curriculum in order to provide children with an identical education. Japanese schools make sure that every student receives the same opportunities so fewer children will fall behind. Unlike the educational system in Japan, individual states in US determine their own curriculum, whereas the federal government decides on teaching content, teaching method, and teaching materials. Schools in America have 第10行 autonomy as well as responsibility for students' learning. Therefore, the quality of education differs. Schools in wealthier districts can provide students with more resources, such as modern classrooms, updated textbooks, experienced teachers and extracurricular activities. However, inner-city schools with smaller budgets cannot give their students the same things.

　　A second difference between Japanese and American schools is the time that students spend 第15行 in school. A typical American school closes for two and a half months in the summer as well as various national holidays. On average, a Japanese student will spend two months more in a classroom than an American counterpart. According to some estimates, in 13 years of schooling, US students receive almost a year less than those in Japan. The implications show that the average school day is longer in Japan, so students have the advantage in practice, repetition, and 第20行 breadth of knowledge. Also, they may retain their lessons during shorter vacation periods.

　　Aside from the curricular and schooling differences, school expense is another aspect distinguishing the educational system of these two countries. The US spends a considerable amount of money on education relative to Japan. Much of the funds are used for things other than academic purposes, including funds for transportation, food, athletics or custodians. In 第25行 contrast, most Japanese students walk or ride their bicycles to school and many traditional

178　Way to go

Japanese schools ask students to clean the school at the end of each day. Moreover, although students in Japan can participate in extracurricular activities like sports after school, most are allowed to choose only one club.

第30行　It may be challenging and difficult to compare the schools of two nations when the nations are significantly <u>dissimilar</u> in various ways. US schools have to deal with issues that Japanese schools do not, and vice versa. If every country was able to choose positive aspects of other countries and successfully implement them into their own societies, each student may reach their potential in the future.

💡單字策略——單字猜測技巧

　　看文章的時候，如果遇到不會的單字，可以用下面幾個步驟來幫助你猜測出單字的意思。首先，先檢視不會的單字找出它的詞性及可能的意思，你可以使用字尾來幫助猜測。例如：-ful, -ive, -able 代表形容詞，-ment, -ness, -ity 代表名詞，-ize, -fy 代表動詞等。再來，找出句子中可能幫助猜測的線索，例如："　，" 同位格的標點符號代表補充說明，"like" 及 "such as" 代表舉例說明。而在 "as well as" 這個片語前面及後面的兩個字詞則會有相似的概念。

A. Read the article again and match the words with their Chinese meanings

1. autonomy
2. resources
3. dissimilar
4. counterpart
5. distinguish
6. fund
7. custodian
8. extracurricular

a. 不同的
b. 區別
c. 資金
d. 課外
e. 資源
f. 自主
g. 相應對的人或物
h. 守衛

Vocabulary

💡單字策略——拆字法

試著將下面的單字拆開，你可以從部份的單字猜出這個單字的意思嗎？

1. resource = re- 一再 + source 來源 → 一再的來源 → 資源

2. autonomy = auto- 自己的；自動的 → 自治

3. dissimilar = dis- 否定 + similar 相似的 → 不相似的 → 不相同的

4. counterpart = counter 相反的 + part 部分 → 配對物；對應的人或物

5. extracurricular = extra- 外加的；額外的 + curricular 課程的 → 課程以外的 → 課外的

單字表

1. curriculum [kə`rɪkjələm]	(n)課程	例 Before we enter a program to study, we had better know the curriculum of the program.
2. federal [`fɛdərəl]	(adj)聯邦政府的	例 The Federal Government of America decides many important policies for this country.
3. autonomy [ɔ`tɑnəmɪ]	(n)自主；自治	例 Students need to develop autonomy for their own learning.
4. resource [rɪ`sors]	(n)資源	例 We need to make good use of natural resources.
5. dissimilar [dɪ`sɪmələ]	(adj)不相同的	例 Although they look similar, the twins are quite dissimilar in their talents.
6. counterpart [`kauntə‚part]	(n)相對應的人或物；配對物	例 When we compare the schools in America and Japan, the schools in America are the counterparts of the schools in Japan.
7. estimate [`ɛstə‚met]	(v)估計	例 The school board estimated the number of freshmen at about 1,200.
8. implication [‚ɪmplɪ`keʃən]	(n)含意；言外之意	例 When we read a novel, sometimes we need to notice the implications behind the words.
9. distinguish [dɪ`stɪŋgwɪʃ]	(v)區別	例 Can you distinguish horses from donkeys?
10. considerable [kən`sɪdərəbl]	(adj)大量的	例 That boy made a considerable change after he entered high school.

11. fund [fʌnd]	(n)資金	例 The church is going to raise funds for the poor.
12. academic [ˌækəˈdɛmɪk]	(adj)學術的	例 The professor devoted himself to the academic world.
13. purpose [ˈpɝpəs]	(n)目的	例 What is the purpose of your visit to the US?
14. custodian [kʌsˈtodɪən]	(n)守衛	例 Custodians are in charge of school safety.
15. extracurricular [ˌɛkstrəkəˈrɪkjələ]	(adj)課外的	例 He likes to participate in extracurricular activities.
16. challenging [ˈtʃælɪndʒ]	(adj)有挑戰性的	例 This task is vey challenging for the employees.
17. vice versa [vaɪs vɝ sɑ]	(adv)反之亦然	例 Parents like their children, and vice versa.
18. implement [ˈɪmpləmənt]	(v)實施	例 Money is needed to implement this project.

💡單字策略──結構性複習

　　當你背完單字的時候，需要一再複習這些單字，才不容易忘記。你知道複習的時間需要間隔多久嗎？背完單字後間隔 15 分鐘以內馬上複習這些單字一次，再過一小時複習第二次，再過三小時複習第三次，再過一天複習第四次，之後，相隔兩天再複習第五次，依照這樣的模式，複習次數越多，中間區隔的時間就可以拉長。

A. Check your review for the following words

Vocabulary	15 min.	1 hour	3 hours	1 day	2 days	1 week	2 weeks
1. curriculum							
2. incorporate							
3. determine							
4. federal							
5. estimate							
6. implication							
7. academic							
8. implement							

Grammar

Contrast signals 對比關係：當我們要比較事物的不同點，可以使用不同字詞及結構來表達。常用的單字有 differ, different, difference, unlike, whereas, in contrast 等。

1. America and Japan school structures <u>differ in</u> many styles of education.

2. <u>The most significant difference</u> is the curriculum design between these two countries.

3. <u>Unlike</u> the educational system in Japan, individual states in US determine their own curriculum, <u>whereas</u> the federal government decides on teaching content, teaching method, and teaching materials.

4. <u>A second difference</u> between Japanese and American schools is the time that students spend in school

5. <u>Aside from the curricular and schooling differences</u>, school expense is another aspect distinguishing the educational system of these two countries.

6. <u>In contrast</u>, most Japanese students walk or ride their bicycles to school and many traditional Japanese schools ask students to clean the school at the end of each day.

常用的對比關係句型有：

1. A and B differ in ...

2. The difference is ...

3. Unlike ... , ...

4. A difference between A and B is ...

5. Aside from ... difference, ... is another aspect distinguishing ...

6. In contrast, ...

其他表示對比關係的常用字有：

Sentence connectors （承轉詞）	1. In contrast
	2. On the other hand
	3. However
	4. On the contrary
	5. Conversely

Coordinating conjunctions (對等連接詞)	1. But 2. Yet
Subordinating conjunctions (從屬連接詞)	1. While 2. Whereas 3. Although 4. Even though
Others (其他)	1. Different from 2. Unlike 3. Differ (from) (in)

Writing

A. Choose an education level and conduct an online search. List the differences between Taiwan and US educational systems at this level.

(*Suggested Website: Ministry of Education http://english.moe.gov.tw/mp.asp?mp=1*)

1. Curriculum

   Points: _____

   _____

   _____

2. Teaching material

   Points: _____

   _____

   _____

3. Explanation

   Points: _____

   _____

   _____

Sentence Patterns

比較相同點	比較不同點
1. similarly	1. in contrast
2. likewise	2. on the other hand
3. also	3. however
4. as	4. but
5. similar to	5. yet
6. equal to	6. while
7. the same as	7. different from
8. like	8. differ (from) (in)

B. Choose an education level and use the outline and sentence patterns above to explain differences between Taiwanese and US educational systems at this level.

_____

_____

_____

_____

_____

_____

_____

Speaking

💡口說策略——條列式將英文說得有條理

　　當你在論述自己意見的時候，可以把想要講的要點條列寫下來，這樣可以幫助你表達的時候更為順暢。

A. If you would like to pursue further study after college education, which one would you prefer, studying in Taiwan or studying in the USA? Think about the advantages and disadvantages and make a list for each of them.

Study in Taiwan		Study in USA	
Advantages	Disadvantages	Advantages	Disadvantages

如何將要點說得更有條理

當你在論述自己意見的時候,可以使用條列式的字當作每一個重點的連接用語。例如:first, firstly, at first, first of all; second, secondly, moreover, furthermore; third, thirdly, in addition, in addition to; finally, lastly 等表示排序性的字眼可以讓你所要表達的意見更爲清楚。

B. State your opinions according to the outlines you make above.

Listening

聽力策略——擷取重點

聽長篇大論的時候需要篩選重要的資訊,例如 people(注意文章中提到的人),objects(注意文章中做的事情或是物品),places(注意文章中的地點),time and numbers(注意文章提到的時間及數字),reasons(注意文章中的因果字詞,例如 because, so 等),ways or methods(注意文章提到對於方法的解釋)等重要的訊息。

以下為聽力內容參考單字:

1. behalf [bɪ`hæf] (n) 代表;利益	4. reform [ˌrɪ`fɔrm] (v) 改革,革新,改良
2. Ministry of Education [`mɪnɪstrɪ ʌv ˌɛdʒʊ`keʃən] (n) 教育部	5. committee [kə`mɪtɪ] (n) 委員會
3. transform [træns`fɔrm] (v) 改造;改革;改善	6. Executive Yuan [ɪg`zɛkjʊtɪv jʊ`ɑn] (n) 行政院

7. era(n) [ˋɪrə] 時代；年代；歷史時期	15. methodology [ˌmɛθədˋɑlədʒɪ] (n) 方法論
8. implementation [ˌɪmpləmɛnˋteʃən] (n) 履行；完成；成就	16. foundation[faʊnˋdeʃən] (n) 建立；創辦
9. specialize [ˋspɛʃəlˌaɪz] (v) 專攻；專門從事	17. specialist(n) [ˋspɛʃəlɪst] 專家
10. contribution [ˌkɑntrəˋbjuʃən] (n) 貢獻	18. ultimate [ˋʌltəmɪt] (adj) 最後的；最終的
11. workforce [wɝk fors] (n) 力，力量；力氣	19. mold [mold] (v) 塑造，把⋯塑造成
12. competition [ˌkɑmpəˋtɪʃən] (n) 競爭；角逐	20. employment(n) [ɪmˋplɔɪmənt] 職業，工作
13. technological [tɛknəˋlɑdʒɪkl] (adj) 技術（學）的，工藝（學）的	21. qualification [ˌkwɑləfəˋkeʃən] (n) 資格，能力
14. vocational [voˋkeʃənl] (adj) 職業的	22. competitiveness [kəmˋpɛtətɪvnɪs] (n) 競爭力

 Track 36

A. Listen to the following lecture and take notes

What	When
The education reform evaluation committee was organized by the Executive Yuan	
The Executive Yuan organized an educational reform promotion team to work on implementing suggestions.	
The Educational Reform Action Program of the Ministry of Education (MOE) was approved by the Executive Yuan which provided a special budget of $5 billion US dollars.	

 Track 37

B. Listen to the following lecture and answer the questions

_____ 1. What did the Technological and Vocational Education Reform Project aim at?

(A) Improving the educational system in general

(B) Enhancing students' general knowledge

(C) Improving theoretical aspects of technological education

(D) Enhancing students' specialized skills

_____ 2. What did the technological and vocational education make in the past?

   (A) It made significant contributions to the country.

   (B) It made no contribution to the country.

   (C) It made very little progress in the educational system.

   (D) It trained academic specialists of various levels.

_____ 3. What are the objectives of technological and vocational reform project?

   (A) Improving teaching and learning environments

   (B) Bridging the gap between business needs and students' abilities

   (C) Training students to become academic specialists in research fields

   (D) Increase the needs of specialists in industries

_____ 4. According to the passage, what is the ultimate goal of the project?

   (A) To mold teaching to meet the demands of industry

   (B) To train students for research need

   (C) To increase the need of job markets

   (D) To arouse employers' responsibilities

ESP

Working as a children's English teacher in a cram school

As a children's English teacher, one has to handle classroom management in the class.

A. Learn some Classroom English

1. It's time for class.

2. Now I am going to call the roll.

3. Who is absent today?

4. Let's start our lesson now.

5. Where did we stop last time?

6. Hand in your homework.

7. Let's review ... first.

8. Today, we're going to learn Lesson ... .

9. Listen carefully.

10. Please underline ...

11. Repeat after me.

12. Read the first paragraph.

13. What's the answer to Item number ...

14. Use English. Say it in English.

15. Let's listen to the CD now.

16. Turn to page ...

17. You did a good job. Good job.

18. Let's give him a big hand.

19. You've made a lot of progress.

20. Louder, please.

21. Don't make any noise.

22. Be quiet.

23. Stop talking.

24. We'll stop here.

25. We'll continue our lesson next time.

B. Read the following articles introducing classroom management

Annoying Classroom Distractions

How can a teacher prevent students' annoying behavior in the classroom? Read the following suggestions:

1. The students and teacher should discuss and adopt acceptable classroom rules by the end of the first week of school.

2. Frequently review the rules of the classroom until the students can successfully obey them.

3. Use simple verbal warnings when misbehaviors occur. Make sure that they are to the point and moderate in tone, like "Stop talking and work on your ... , please").

4. Give praise to the class frequently, like "Thank you for working so quietly," or "I'm pleased to see you all working so well today."

5. Intervene the misbehavior as soon as possible before it is too late. For example, the teacher may say "May I help you with your assignment?" when the student begins to show signs of frustration.

6. Use facial expressions to let students know that the misbehavior was not totally ignored.

7. Talk to students in private to know the reasons for their misbehaviors.

8. Encourage students to strive for greater self-control.

9. Contact parents or administrators when there is no other ways to resolve the conflict situation.

10. Refer students to appropriate staff members. Keep records to support your concerns.

C. Choose one situation below. State how you will handle the situation.

Situation 1: One of the students keeps talking in class with his/her peers.

Situation 2: One of the students cheats in a quiz.

Situation 3: One of the students fails to finish his/her assignments.

Situation 4: Two students work in a pair, but start fighting.

Student Book Answer Keys

Unit 1 Movie

Warm up

    A. Answers may vary

    B. 1. Write out the script   2. Choose the cast   3. Design the costume

        4. Shoot the film   5. Edit the film   6. Add the sound effects

Vocabulary

Cast	Script	Film shooting	Film editing
actor, actress, director, character	screenwriter, screen play	cameraman, scene, lighting designer	film editor, sound editor

Reading

    A. 1. Possible answers: John thinks the movie is great. The story and the scenes are good.

          (Words/phrases: great, like, love, nice and touching story, scenes are so colorful

          and beautiful.)

    B. Answers may vary.

Grammar

B. When there is _____X_____ Hollywood, there is _____X_____ Bollywood.

_____X_____ Bollywood is the name used for _____the_____ film industry in

_____X_____ India, _____a_____ country near _____the_____ Indian Ocean.

_____X_____ Bollywood is _____the_____ largest film producer in India and

one of _____the_____ largest centers of film production in _____the_____ world.

_____X_____ Bollywood movies are mostly musicals. They are often presented with

_____X_____ songs and dance. _____A_____ film's success often depends on

the quality of _____the_____ songs and dance. _____A_____ film's music is often

released before the movie itself and helps get more people to know about it.

Writing

    A. Answers may vary

Speaking

    B. 2. The house around the corner is new.

        3. Beauty is in the eye of the beholder.

        4. Life is like a ladder, the higher you climb, the more expansive your view is.

Listening

    A. Disagree. Reason: The woman really loves the movie but the man thinks the story didn't touch his heart.

   B. Agree. Both the man and the woman love the settings and the actions of the movie.

ESP

   A. 1. c   2. j   3. h   4. a   5. b   6. f   7. e   8. i   9. d   10. g

---

Unit 1   Audioscript

Track 1

Unit 1 Speaking Part A. **Listen and practice saying the sounds out loud.**

   a [ə] or [æ]

   an [ən] or [æn]

   the [ðə] or [ðɪ]

Track 2

Unit 1 Speaking Part B. **Practice reading the sentences out loud. Mark the linking sounds.**

   1. An apple a day keeps the doctor away.

   2. The house around the corner is new.

   3. Beauty is in the eye of the beholder.

   4. Life is like a ladder, the higher you climb, the more expansive your view is.

Track 3

Unit 1 Speaking Part C. **Listen and check if the linking sounds you marked are correct. Then practice reading the sentences aloud with your partner.**

Track 4

Unit 1 Listening Part A. **Listen to people talking about a famous movie - Avatar. Do they agree or disagree with each other? Why? Circle the correct answer and write down the reason.**

Avatar

Woman: Have you watched "Avatar" yet?

   Man: Oh, yeah.

Woman: Oh! I really love it. I'm so surprised at the 3D effects.

   Man: The effects are good but the story isn't good enough. It doesn't touch my heart.

Woman: Maybe the ending isn't good enough but I never found myself being bored when watching this movie.

Unit 1 Listening Part B. **Listen to people talking about one more movie. Do they agree or disagree with each other? Why? Circle the correct answer and write down the reason.**

The Twilight Saga: New moon

Man: I just watched the movie "The Twilight Saga: New moon" on DVD.

Woman: What do you think about it?

Man: I love the settings and the actions.

Woman: Oh, yes! I especially love the characters. They are so handsome and beautiful.

Unit 2   Hotel

Warm up

A. 1. c   2. f   3. d   4. b   5. e   6. g   7. h

Extra word: to book (to arrange a room, table, seat ... etc. with a hotel, restaurant, theater on a particular date).

Reading

A. 1. Sun Inn   2. Lakeside Hotel   3. Lakeside Hotel   4. Sun Inn

   5. Lakeside Hotel   6. Lakeside Hotel   7. Sun Inn

Grammar

A. 1. 說話者可能或期望在Sun Inn 待兩晚，這有可能是說話者在說話當下所做的一個決定。

   2. 說話者意圖並計畫在Sun Inn 待兩晚。

   3. 說話者安排在Sun Inn 待兩晚，說話者非常確定這個動作會執行。

B. Answers may vary.

Writing

A. 1. I would (I'd) prefer a standard guest room/ a suite.

   2. I would (I'd) prefer taking a bus.

   3. Would you prefer to take a trip to Sun Moon Lake or to Kenting?

   4. Answers may vary.

Speaking

B. Answers may vary.

C. Answers may vary.

D. Answers may vary.

Listening

A.

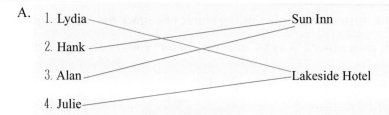

1. Lydia ———————————————— Sun Inn

2. Hank ——————————————

3. Alan ———————————————— Lakeside Hotel

4. Julie ——————————

B.

	Room type	Check-in time	Check-out time
1. Lydia	*standard guest room*	2 pm	11 am
2. Hank	twin room	2 pm	12 pm
3. Alan	suite	12 pm	10 am
4. Julie	double room	11 am	10 am

Unit 2   Audioscript

Track 6

Unit 2 Speaking Part A. Pronunciation. Listen and Practice.

   1. I'd prefer the Sun Inn.

   2. I'd prefer staying in the Lakeview Hotel.

   3. I'd prefer to use a pencil.

Track 7

Unit 2 Listening Part A. Hotel room booking. Listen to people calling to book hotel rooms. Would they prefer the Sun Inn or the Lakeside Hotel? Match the names with the correct hotel. The first one has been done for you.

1. **Lydia**

   R: Lakeside Hotel. How may I help you?

   L: I'm going to travel to Sun Moon Lake next week. I want to book a room for a night.

   R: What type of room would you prefer?

   L: A standard guest room is good.

   R: Okay. A standard guest room for a night. May I have your name, please?

   L: Lydia Baker. Oh! When is the check-in time?

   R: It's 2 pm. And the check-out time is 11 in the morning.

2. **Hank**

   H: Is this the Sun Inn?

   R: Yes, how may I help you?

   H: I'd like to reserve two rooms for this Saturday night.

   R: What kind of room would you prefer?

H: We have 8 people. Do you have twin rooms?

R: Yes, we do. So, two twin rooms for you?

H: That's right.

R: May I have your name?

H: Hank, Hank White.

R: Ok. Mr. White. We have reserved 2 twin rooms for you. And please check in after 2 pm and check out by 12 the next day. Thank you for calling.

3. **Alan**

R: This is the Sun Inn room booking service. How can I help you?

A: I'd like to book two nights for this weekend. I'm going on a business trip.

R: We only have a lakeview suite for this weekend.

A: Mm~ That's fine. I'll book it. When can I check in?

R: The check-in time is at 12 noon.

A: And the check-out time?

R: It's 10 in the morning. Can I have your name, please?

A: It's Alan Brown.

4. **Julie**

R: Lakeside Hotel front desk. May I help you?

J: Are there rooms available for next weekend?

R: Yes, there are. What type of room would you prefer?

J: I'd prefer a double room.

R: Ok! One double room. Is the booking for one or two nights?

J: Two, please.

R: Ok. The room has been booked for you, and may I ask you to check in after 11:00 AM on Friday and check out before 10:00 AM on Sunday?

J: Sure, no problem.

R: Great! May I have your name, please?

J: Julie. Julie Foster.

Track 8

Unit 2 Listening Part B. **Listen to Part A again. Complete the chart.**

Unit 3　Food
Warm up

A.

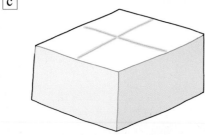

B. Sounds are like Chinese translations

Vocabulary

Appetizer / Cold Dish	Main Dish	Soup	Dessert	Beverage
green salad	stir-fried chicken noodles	wonton soup	pudding	chocolate shakes
potato skins	cheeseburger	hot and sour soup	doughnut	black tea
dried tofu	dumplings			green tea
cucumber salad	hot dog			coke

Reading

A. Answers may vary

B. 1. (A)　2. (C)　3. (B)

C. (1) Yummy is cheaper than Dali.　(2) She needs to spend $ 220 in total.

Writing

    A. Answers may vary.

Speaking

    A. Answers may vary.

    B. Answers may vary.

Listening

    C.

Dali's All-You-Can-Eat Menu
Cold Dish
☑ Dried tofu   ☐ Cucumber salad
Stir-fried Vegetable
☑ Water spinach   ☐ Eggplants
Main Dish
☑ Stir-fried chicken noodles   ☐ Dumplings

    D. 1. (A)   2. (B)   3. (D)

Unit 3 Audioscript

Track 9

Unit 3 Listening Part A. Let's practice the following sounds.

    1. come on [kʌmɑn]

    2. have a seat [hævə]

Track 10

Unit 3 Listening Part B. Practice the sentences below.

    1. I hope you like it.   2. Let's find a burger place.

    3. That's a good idea.   4. I want to have a pudding.

    5. That's a total of NT$400.

Track 11

Unit 3 Listening Part C. Listen to the dialogue and check the dishes they are talking about.

John: Come on, Jean. Have a seat.

Jean: OK!

John: This is my favorite restaurant. I believe you'll like it.

Jean: I hope so!

John: OK, what do you want to eat?

Jean: Hmm.

John: Let's get some dried tofu!

Jean: What's that? I have never heard of that before.

John: It's very tasty! You should try some.

Jean: Oh! Go ahead! You can order it if you want.

John: How about some vegetables? Stir-fried water spinach is yummy.

Jean: I've never tried that before, either. We can give it a try.

John: How about the main dish? I love stir-fried chicken noodles.

Jean: Hmm~ Actually, I don't like that kind of food.

John: Ok. What would you like?

Jean: Do you think they have hot dogs or hamburgers?

John: Jean! We are in a Chinese restaurant!

Jean: But I told you I want to eat American food! I think potato skins are more delicious than dried tofu and stir-fried vegetables. Cheeseburgers are more flavorsome than chicken noodles.

John: Well, maybe next time, we will find a burger place.

Track 12

Unit 3 Listening Part D. **Listen to the dialogue again and choose the correct answer.**

Unit 4　Travel & Flight

Warm up

 A. 1. b 2. e 3. a 4. d 5. h 6. g 7. i 8. c 9. f 10. j

Reading

 A. New York

 B. 1. 13:05 2. Terminal 3 3. January 8th, 2013

   4. Boeing 747 5. the economy class 6. No

   7. 14 hours and 35 minutes

Listening

 A. In an airport

 B. 1. In an airport; key words: flight, boarding gate, begin boarding.

   2. In a department store; key words: customer, customer service section.

   3. In an airport; key words: Formosa Airway's passenger, Gate 10.

   4. On a train; key words: Taipei station, mind the gap, get off the train.

Writing

Arrival Record
Admission Number
491755175 21

1. Family Name
   CHEN

2. First (Given) Name
   AMY

3. Birth Date (DD/MM/YY)
   20031990

4. Country of Citizenship
   REPUBLIC OF CHINA

5. Sex (Male or Female)
   FEMALE

6. Passport Issue Date (DD/MM/YY)
   05052008

7. Passport Expiration Date (DD/MM/YY)
   05052018

8. Passport Number
   223411003

9. Airline and Flight Number
   U745

10. Country Where You Live
    REPUBLIC OF CHINA

11. Country Where You Boarded
    JAPAN

12. City Where Visa Was Issued
    TAIPEI

13. Date Issued (DD/MM/YY)
    14072012

14. Address While in the United States (Number and Street)

15. City and State

16. Telephone Number in the U.S. Where You can be Reached

17. Email Address

DEPARTMENT OF HOMELAND SECURITY

U.S. Customs and Border Protection

Departure Record
Admission Number
491755175 21

18. Family Name
    CHEN

19. First (Given) Name
    AMY

20. Birth Date (DD/MM/YY)
    20031990

21. Country of Citizenship
    REPUBLIC OF CHINA

Grammar

   B. 1. Can you tell me if/whether Broadway is around here?

   2. Could you tell me if/whether Central Park is near Times Square?

   3. Do you know where the Statue of Liberty is?

   4. Do you know how far Yankee Stadium is?

   5. Can you tell me what is special on Wall Street?

Unit 4   Audioscript

Track 13

Unit 4 Listening Part A. Listen to the announcement. Where can you hear this announcement? Circle the correct place.

Attention, please. Attention, please. Passengers on flight Z908 departing for Taipei, please proceed to Gate 16 to begin boarding. Thank you.

Track 14

Unit 4 Listening Part B. Listen to four announcements. Write down the key words that you hear. Circle the correct place where you can hear these announcements.

   1. Passengers on flight A867 departing for Tokyo. The boarding gate has been changed to 9B. And there will be a slight delay because of the bad weather conditions. We hope to begin boarding in 20 minutes. Thank you for your patience.

   2. Customer, Ms, Janet Lee, please come to the customer service section on the first floor. Your friends are waiting for you here.

   3. Formosa Airway's passenger, Mr. David, Jin and Ms. Carol, Lo. Please immediately proceed to Gate 10. The gate is about to close and we are ready to depart now.

   4. We are now approaching Taipei station. Passengers please mind the gap when you get off the train. The next stop is Taoyuan.

Unit 5   Clothes

Warm up

   1. b   2.c   3.a

Vocabulary

上衣類	褲子類
T-shirt blouse shirt jacket overcoat	jeans shorts trousers slacks leggings

Reading

A.

Jacket	Overcoat	Leggings	Blouse
☑ ironed	☒ ironed	☑ ironed	☑ ironed
☑ washed by machines	☒ washed by machines	☑ washed by machines	☑ washed by machines
☒ bleached	☒ bleached	☒ bleached	☑ bleached
☒ tumble dried	☒ tumble dried	☒ soaked	☑ tumble dried
Made in USA	Made in USA	Made in Taiwan	Made in China

Grammar

A. 現在簡單被動式→ S +am/is/are + PP + by + O

過去簡單被動式→ S + was/were +PP + by + O

未來簡單被動式→ S + will +be + PP +by + O

Writing

Answers may vary.

Speaking

A. 1. one hundred and twenty five US dollars

2. two hundred and forty-eight NT dollars

3. three thousand five hundred and twenty-four Japanese Yen

4. eight thousand nine hundred and forty-six Thai Baht

B. Answers may vary

Listening

A. 1. THB $ 1,000.　2. TWD $ 1,460.　3. USD $ 117.　4. JPY $5,818.　5. USD $ 90.

6. THB $516.　7. JPY $9,880.　8. THB $330.　9. TWD $6,616.　10. USD $ 40.

11. THB $515.　12. JPY $660.　13. USD $17.　14. THB$718.　15. JPY $8,419.

B. 1. (B)　2. (A)　3. (D)　4. (B)

Unit 5　Audioscript

Track 15

Unit 5 Listening Part A. **Listen to the statements and take notes on the prices. The first one has been done for you.**

1. The blouse costs THB $ 1,000.　　2. The T-shirt costs TWD $ 1,460.

3. The jacket costs USD $ 117.　　4. The jeans cost JPY $5,818.

5. The leggings cost USD $ 90.　　6. The slacks cost THB $516.

7. The trousers cost JPY $9,880.　　8. The shorts cost THB $330.

9. The overcoat costs TWD $6,616.　　10. The shirt costs USD $ 40.

11. The pants cost THB $515.   12. The blouse costs JPY $660.

14. The leggings cost THB$718.   13. The T-shirt costs USD $17.

15. The overcoat costs JPY $8,419.

Unit 5 Listening Part B. **Listen to the dialogue and choose the correct answer.**

Customer: I like that gray blouse very much, but I don't think I can afford it! It's too expensive for me.

Clerk: Let me check the price for you. I think it's on sale. It's 30 percent off! It will only come to nine hundred and ninety THB with the discount.

Customer: Hmm ... 30 percent off. That's a little bit better, but it still costs too much for me!

Clerk: Let me show you other blouses. I think we have similar styles on sale. Take a look at this one. It's light gray. It just costs five hundred and ninety-nine THB.

Customer: Hmm! This price sounds reasonable. Let me take a look at the labels inside. Oh! It's made in Vietnam and it's made of 50% cotton and 50% Polyester.

Clerk: Yes! It's very good quality, but be sure to hand wash it only. Don't bleach or tumble dry it.

Unit 6   Health

Warm up (Answer may vary)

A.

Symptom	Symptom
Possible sicknesses	Possible sicknesses
Common cold, flu	Common cold, flu
Symptoms	Symptoms

Possible sickness	Possible sicknesses
Common cold, flu	Common cold, flu
Symptoms	**Symptoms**
Possible sicknesses	Possible sicknesses
Common cold, flu, asthma	Common cold, flu, asthma

Vocabulary

(Answers may vary)

單字編成故事：tobacco（菸草）→trigger（引起）→sneeze（鼻涕）& asthma（氣喘）→symptom（徵兆）→需要inhale（吸入）→nasal spray（鼻子噴劑）→服用pill（藥片）及注射vaccine（疫苗）

Reading

A. 1. (C)　　2. (B)　　3. (B)

B. 1. I should take antibiotics, get plenty of rest, drink plenty of fluids, and use sore throat spray or nasal spray to relieve the symptoms.

　　2. I should get a flu vaccine, wash my hands with soap and water, keep away from sick people, and avoid crowds.

　　3. The symptoms for the asthma may be breathlessness, chest tightness, and nighttime or early morning coughing.

Writing

A. Answers may vary

Speaking

A. Answers may vary

B. 1. double five eight nine six eight　　2. seven triple four eight two

　　3. one two double three five six　　4. eight double five double eight four

　　5. six five double zero (double O) three five

Listening

A. 1. □ It's 5:35 / ☑ It's 3: 53　　3. ☑ It's 9:17 / □ It's 7:19

　　2. ☑ It's 8:40 / □ It's 4:08

B. 1. It's 5: 22　　2. It's 6:16

C. 1. (A)   2. (C)   3. (C)

Unit 6   Audioscript

Track 17

Unit 6 Listening Part A. Listen to the time expressions and select the correct time below.

  1. It's 3:53. 2. It's 8:40. 3. It's 9: 17.

Track 18

Unit 6 Listening Part B. Listen to the time expressions and write down the time below.

  1. It's 5: 22. 2. It's 6:16.

Track 19

Unit 6 Listening Part C. Listen to the dialogue and answer the questions.

Nurse: This is HEALTH CLINIC. How may I help you?

Patient: Yes, I'd like to register to see Dr. Tom Wilson this coming Friday.

Nurse: OK! Hold on please. Let me check. May I have your ID number?

Patient: Yes, it's A549887264.

Nurse: A-5-4-9-double 8-7-2-6-4. Is that correct?

Patient: That's right.

Nurse: OK, so you are Mr. Lin, right?

Patient: Yes!

Nurse: Your number is 19. Dr. Wilson will see you at about 9:15 this coming Friday. Please be on time.

Patient: Oh! That is too early for me. I won't get there until 9:30 this coming Friday.

Nurse: Let me check. All right! How about 9:45?

Patient: I think that would be more convenient for me.

Nurse: Then your number is changed from 19 to 36.

Patient: Number 36! OK! Thank you very much.

Nurse: You're welcome.

Unit 7   Living Green

Warm up

  A. 2. DOs 3. DON'Ts 4. DOs 5. DOs 6. DOs 7. DON'Ts 8. DOs

   9. DOs

Grammar

可數與不可數名詞：

A.

可數名詞	不可數名詞
an assistant a horse a computer a dollar	tea wood rice tennis reality anger

B. 1. green tea　2. information　3. a newspaper　4. patience　5. a dollar

現在簡單式與未來式複習：

A. 1. Present continuous　2. Present simple

B. 1. (B)　2. (B)　3. (B)　4. (A)

Listening

B. 1. (B)　2. (A)　3. (B)　4. (B)

ESP

B. 1. d　2. b　3. a　4. f　5. e　6. c

Unit 7　Audioscript

Track 20

Unit 7 Listening Part A. **Listen to the talk. Take notes when you listen.**

Many countries are looking for new sources of energy and Japan has found one. Japanese collect snow in winter to provide energy for their cooling systems at Hokkaido airport in summer. Collecting snow not only provides energy, it also reduces CO_2 production. According to statistics, 30% of energy is saved and 2100 tons of CO_2 is reduced per year. In fact, using snow is not new to Japan. Several other places in Japan have been collecting snow since 1998.

Track 21

Unit 7 Listening Part C. **Listen to Part A again. Check your answers. (Remember to listen for the specific information.)**

Unit 8　Banking

Vocabulary

A. 1. sell → purchase　2. idealistic → realistic　3. objective → goal

Reading

A. 1. To tell you how to save your money

2. (A) Develop a monthly budge: write down the budge for what you spend

(B) Wait before you buy: avoid impulse purchases

(C) Limit spending: Limit unnecessary purchases

(D) Change your lifestyle: Change your lifestyle into simpler ways so as to save more money

Grammar

A. 請依照上面的例句寫出使用意志動詞的公式

It is necessary/important/critical/suggested + that + S + (should) + 原型V

B. 1. (C)   2. (D)   3. (C)   4. (C)   5. (C)

Writing

Answers may vary

Speaking

Answers may vary

Listening

A. 1. Transition word: First

Opinion: keep most of your money in banks

2. Transition word: Second

Opinion: place some of your money in stocks or funds

3. Transition word: Third

Opinion: spend the rest of your money carefully on daily consumption

B. 1. (B)   2. (A)   3. (C)   4. (D)

Unit 8   Audioscript

Track 22

Unit 8 Listening Part A. Listen to the following reports for opinions and take notes on each of them.

1. first, it is important that you keep most of your money in banks

2. Second, it is essential that you place some of your money in stocks or funds.

3. Finally, it is critical that you spend the rest of your money carefully on daily consumption.

Unit 8 Listening Part B. **Listen to the following dialogue and choose the correct answer.**

Broadcaster: Now let's take another call. Hi! Welcome to the CJC broadcast. What's your name?

Caller: Keller!

Broadcaster: Hi! Keller! Tell us your opinion on using credit cards.

Caller: As far as I am concerned, there are three reasons for me to avoid using credit cards. First of all, my mother insists that I buy more things than I need if I use a credit card. I may use money without control and buy things that I don't need. Secondly my father demands that I be responsible and pay every payment on time. Otherwise, if I delay a payment, I will have to pay extra fees or even penalty charges. Finally, my friend suggests that I keep my credit card in a safe place. If my card is lost or stolen, there is the danger of credit card fraud. In this case, I need to make a huge payment for somebody else. All in all, using a credit card could bring me a lot of inconvenience, so I prefer to use cash.

Broadcast: OK! Thanks for your opinion! It seems that credit cards could bring you financial chaos, but anyway, thanks for your call. Now let's welcome the next call~ Hi!

Unit 9　Common Courtesy

Warm up

　　A. Answers may vary

Reading

　　A. 1. (D)　2. (C)　3. (D)　4. (A)

　　B. 1. T　2. T　3. F

Grammar

　　A. 1. (C)　2. (A)　3. (D)　4. (B)　5. (D)

Writing

　　A. (A) Chris <u>parked</u> his scooter in a parking space when he was rushing for a job interview.

　　(B) A car driver wanted to park his car in this space, but he found that a scooter <u>has already occupied</u> this space.

　　(C) The car driver was angry and <u>banged</u> the door against the scooter. This made Chris angry so he argued with the car driver.

　　(D) When Chris stepped into the office for the job interview, he found that the car driver that he argued with was the employer.

B. Possible answers:

For picture 1: Parking the car or motorcycle in the wrong place may cause certain problems. The man should avoid parking his scooter in a parking space.

For picture 2: Occupying the parking lot may cause other people's inconvenience. I recommend that Chris should not put his vehicle in this space.

For picture 3: Banging the door against other people's vehicle is very rude. The man should say sorry to Chris.

For picture 4: Attending the job interview is very important. I consider arriving at the place for interviews earlier so that an embarrassing situation will not occur.

Speaking

Answers may vary.

Listening

A. 1. If someone is new to the company or neighborhood, introducing yourself and assisting them can show your kindness. Being sincere and giving a little personal history can make the newcomer feel welcome. Bringing a basket of food is a good way to welcome your new neighbors.

2. Thinking of someone else shows courtesy. Displaying this in your everyday behavior, such as opening the door or a car door for others.

3. Putting food items back is a nice gesture. Everything should have its own home; if you take it out, it's courteous to put it back so that the next person can find it when he or she needs it!

B. 1. (A)   2. (B)   3. (C)   4. (D)

Unit 9   Audioscript

Track 24

Unit 9 Listening Part A. **Listen to the following statements and fill in the blanks**

1. If someone is new to the company or neighborhood, introducing yourself and assisting them can show your kindness. Being sincere and giving a little personal history can make the newcomer feel welcome. Bringing a basket of food is a good way to welcome your new neighbors.

2. Thinking of someone else shows courtesy. Displaying this in your everyday behavior, such as opening the door or a car door for others.

3. Putting food items back is a nice gesture. Everything should have its own home; if

you take it out, it's courteous to put it back so that the next person can find it when he or she needs it!

Track 25

Unit 9 Listening Part B. **Listen to the following statements and choose the correct answer**

1. Obeying traffic rules is a good way to be a courteous driver. You should avoid blocking the exit. It's the right thing to do and it only takes few minutes to be thoughtful and courteous. You should not cause inconvenience for other drivers when you change lanes.

2. Helping the handicapped, elderly, or children who are having difficulty is also a good thing for you to do. Trying to support the disabled or trying to help children find their parents can show your kindness.

3. As the saying goes, "If you don't have something nice to say, don't say anything at all!" Keeping gossip to yourself can keep you out of ugly arguments.

4. Encouraging others to do their best is one way to show your courtesy. Inspiring them when they need it and complimenting them on a good job may encourage your friends to have a positive attitude.

Unit 10   Housing

Warm up

A. Match the picture with its English name

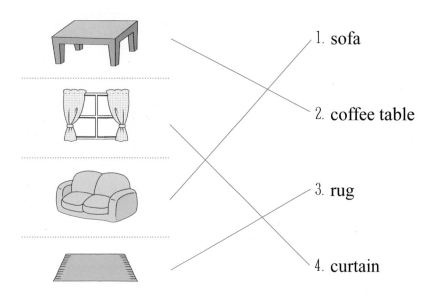

1. sofa

2. coffee table

3. rug

4. curtain

B. Answers may vary.

C. 1. coffee table　2. sofa　3. loveseat　4. armchair　5. throw pillow　6. curtain
　　7. lamp　8. end table　9. rug　10. floor　11. fireplace　12. painting

Reading

A. 1. (B)　2. (B)　3. (A)　4. (D)

Grammar

1.
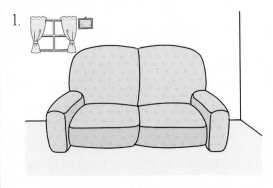
against

4.

in the corner

2.

in front of

5.

next to

3.
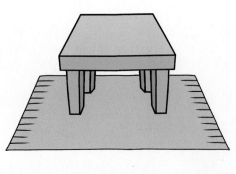
under

6.

on

Writing

Answers may vary.

Speaking

Answers may vary.

Listening

1. ☑

5. ☐

2. ☐

6. ☑

3. ☑

7. ☐

4. ☐

8. ☑

ESP

1. decorating styles   2. color schemes   3. organization

Unit 10   Audioscript

Unit 10 Listening Part A. **Listen to the descriptions and choose the correct picture according to the text.**

1. In this room, you can see a sofa next to an end table. A lamp is on the end table. There is a rug under the end table. A window with curtains is behind the sofa.

2. As you can see in this room, there is a waste can near the desk. A telephone and a fax machine are on the desk. A white board is on the wall. Two chairs are positioned in the corner.

3. In this room, an end table in front of the bed is between two armchairs. Acarpet is under the end table. A loveseat against the window is positioned to the left of the bed. Two throw pillows are on the bed.

4. In this room, a white board against the wall is in front of the round table. Two chairs are positioned at the right side of the table. Another three chairs are at the left side of the table. A plant is in the corner.

Unit 11   Technology

Warm up

A. 18th century (Industrial revolution), 19th century, 20th century, 21st century

Reading

A. Answers may vary.

Vocabulary

A. See glossary (單字表) of the unit.

Manufacture (v): manufactory (n), manufacturable (adj), manufacturer (n), manufactured (adj), manufacturing (n, adj)

Steam (n): steamer (n), steamily (adv), steaminess (n), steamy (adj), steamed (adj)

Electronic (adj): electron (n), electronically (adv), electronics (n)

Improve (v): improved (adj), improvement (n), improver (n), improvability (n), improvable (adj), improvably (adv)

Grammar

A.

Present	Past	Past Participle
break	broke	broken
bring	brought	brought
buy	bought	bought

A.

Present	Past	Past Participle
choose	chose	chosen
drink	drank	drunk
fall	fell	fallen
freeze	froze	frozen
grow	grew	grown
hide	hid	hidden
lead	led	led
lie	lay	lain
ride	rode	ridden
run	ran	run
see	saw	seen
shake	shook	shaken
shine	shone	shone
shoot	shot	shot
steal	stole	stolen
wake	woke	woken
wear	wore	worn

C.

Past simple	◆ completed actions in the past
Present perfect	◆ situations or actions that began in the past and still continue ◆ focusing on the present result of a past action or recent event ◆ referring to situations or actions in a time period up to now

D. 1. (B) 2. (A) 3. (B) 4. (A) 5. (B)

Listening

A. 2. Now I'll move onto the second reason.

3. Next

4. Coming now to my last point

B. Key words: 2. Fun games 3. photo sharing 4. Real-time updates

Sequence (from the top): 2 → 4 → 1 → 3

Unit 11 Audioscript

Track 27

Unit 11 Listening Part A. Listen to a talk about "facebook". Write down the signposting phrases or sequencing phrases that help you understand the structure of the talk.

Are you on facebook yet? Many people nowadays use facebook as their favorite way of keeping in touch with their friends or even making new friends. Why? Today I'm going to

Unit 12　Novel & Music

Reading

A. Possible answers:

Main characters: old man, his son, donkey

Setting: The man, his son and the donkey were going to the market.

Problem: People blame them (laughed at them) on whatever way they used to get to the market.

Story events: The old man rode on the donkey. The son rode on the donkey. The old man and the son rode on the donkey. The old man and the son carried the donkey.

Ending: The donkey died.

Grammar

A.

Causative verbs:	
1. 動詞＋受詞＋to＋原形動詞	2. 動詞＋受詞＋原形動詞
get persuade force order allow permit want	let have make

Note：當受詞被動接受其後所接的動詞時，不管這個causative verb是屬於第一或第二類皆需接過去分詞型態的動詞。

B. 1. (C)　2. (D)　3. (B)　4. (B)　5. (C)

Speaking

A. Possible answers:

2. She should get her hair cut.　3. You can allow him/her to work alone.

4. He can try to persuade them to trust him.　5. She can have someone to repair it.

6. You should get your room cleaned.　7. He should make himself love it.

Listening

A. 1. apart　2. in　3. chairs　4. at　5. back　6. each

7. missed　8. went　9. lied　10. stage　11. if　12. filled

ESP

A. 1. F　2. T　3. F　4. F　5. T

Unit 12　Audioscript

Track 29

Unit 12 Listening Part A. Listen to the song and complete the lyrics.

Are you lonesome tonight

Do you miss me tonight

Are you sorry we drifted apart

Is the memory still in your heart

Are you lonesome tonight

Do you miss me tonight

Are you sorry we drifted apart

Does your memory stray

To a bright summer day

When I kissed you and called you sweetheart

Do the chairs in your parlor

Seem empty and bare

Do you gaze at your doorstep and picture me there

Is your heart filled with pain

Shall I come back again

Tell me dear, are you lonesome tonight

I wonder if you're lonesome tonight

You know someone said the world's a stage

And each must play a part

Fate had me play a lover with you as my sweetheart

Act one was where we met

I loved you at first glance

You read your line so cleverly

And never missed a cue

Then came act two

And you seemed to change

You acted strange

Why? I'll never know

Then came the day

When you went away and left me all alone

If you lied when you said you loved

I had no 'cause to doubt you

But I'd rather go on hearing your lies

Than go on living without you

The stage is bare and I'm standing there

In the part of a broken clown

And if you won't come back to me

Then they can bring the curtain down

Is your heart filled with pain

Shall I come back again

Tell me dear are you lonesome tonight

(Are you lonesome tonight)

Unit 13   Biology

Reading

A. Jet Li: type A

Leonardo Dicaprio: type B

Elvis Presley: type O

Jackie Chan: type AB

Vocabulary

A.

Positive	Negative
reserved	stubborn
patient	forgetful
creative	insensitive
passionate	indecisive
ambitious	
self-confident	
rational	

Vocabulary strategy

1. unreserved   2. impatient   3. uncreative   4. non-passionate   5. non-forgetful

6. unambitious   7. irrational

Grammar

A. 第一句陳述一現在事實；第二及三句則是與現在事實相反的陳述。

B. 1. If S+ past tense, S+ would + base form of a verb.

= S+ would + base form of a verb + if S+ past tense.

2. I wish + S + past tense.

C. Answers may vary.

Listening

A. Lily: type O

B. Johnson: type AB

Ruth: type A

Rod: type B

ESP

1. capsules   2. Direction   3. Description   4. Ingredient   5. Warning

Unit 13   Audioscript

Unit 13 Listening Part A. Listen to a conversation. Guess which blood type Lily has according to the chart.

Lily

A: Do you know Lily?

B: Is she your new classmate?

A: Yes, she's very ambitious. She said she wanted to become the top student in our class.

B: She must be very self-confident too.

A: Oh Yeah! But she is a little insensitive sometimes. She doesn't know she sometimes hurts our feelings.

Unit 13 Listening Part B. Listen to three more conversations. Guess which blood type Johnson, Ruth and Rod have. Write the correct answer next to each picture.

1. **Johnson**

   A: You know what? I met a guy these days. He is so special!

   B: How's he special?

   A: He never cares about what we care about. He's cold!

   B: Hm ...

   A: And, he is a rational person.

   B: That's good.

   A: But he's sometimes indecisive.

   B: That's not so good, then.

2. **Ruth**

   A: You know Lisa? My best friend?

   B: Yeah. You talk about her all the time.

   A: She is so reserved.

   B: You told me last time that she's a patient woman.

   A: Oh, she is. She always listens to me when I complain.

   B: She's a real friend!

   A: The only thing I don't like about her is her stubbornness.

3. **Rod**

   A: How's your son?

Unit 14   Fashion Design

Reading

   A. 1. F   2. F   3. F   4. T   5. T   6. T

Vocabulary

   A. Answers may vary.

Grammar

   A. If + S + had done something, S + would + have done ⋯

   = S + would have done ... if S + had done something.

   B. 1. (C)   2. (D)   3. (B)   4. (A)

Listening

   A. ☑ Where are you from?

   □ Where do you live now?

   ☑ Who supported you to become a designer?

   □ How did you pursue your dream?

   ☑ What inspired you to become a fashion designer?

   □ What are your must-have items?

   ☑ What's your personal style?

   □ What are you wearing right now?

   ☑ When's your first exhibit?

   B. Where are you from? Cecilia is from Taiwan.

   Who supported you to become a designer? Both her parents and high school teacher.

   What inspired you to become a fashion designer? Johan Ku's story.

   What's your personal style? She likes to wear something casual.

   When's your first exhibit? In April.

ESP

   A. 1. b   2. a   3. d   4. e   5. c   6. g   7. j   8. h   9. i   10. f

   B. ___3___ put on some face cream

<u> 1 </u> wash her face

<u> 7 </u> put some blusher on her cheeks

<u> 2 </u> put on some lotion

<u> 6 </u> use a powder puff to put on some powder

<u> 4 </u> put on some make-up base

<u> 5 </u> use a make-up sponge to put on foundation

<u> 9 </u> put on some lipstick

<u> 8 </u> put on some eye shadow

Unit 14 Audioscript

Track 32

Unit 14 Listening Part A. **Listen to the interview with another famous fashion designer, Cecilia Lee. "What are the interview questions?" Check the questions that you hear.**

Interviewer: Today, we're very lucky to have Cecilia Lee, an award-winning designer, to join us on the air. Let's welcome Cecilia!

Cecilia: Hi, nice to meet you.

Interviewer: Nice to meet you, too. Mm⋯ Cecilia, where are you from?

Cecilia: I'm originally from Taiwan but now I live in France.

Interviewer: You're a very successful fashion designer now. Who supported you to become a designer?

Cecilia: Both of my parents and my high school teacher especially. My parents have never forced me to do anything that I am not interested in. I make my own decisions most of the time. They just give me suggestions. I had a chance to study law but I knew that I wouldn't like it. If my parents had forced me to study law, I wouldn't have listened to my heart.

Interviewer: And your high school teacher?

Cecilia: She recognized my art talent and encouraged me to go for it. If she hadn't encouraged me, I wouldn't have studied fashion and textile design at university.

Interviewer: What inspired you to become a fashion designer?

Cecilia: Johan Ku's story. I read about his story and realized that we didn't need to be born in a rich family. We could be very successful if only we worked hard and never gave up.

Interviewer: What's your personal style?

Cecilia: I like something that's casual like a T-shirt and jeans.

Interviewer: When's your first exhibit?

Cecilia: Most of my collections will be exhibited at the Fine Art Museum in April.

Track 33

Unit 14 Listening Part B. Listen to Part A again. Answer the questions that you've checked.

Unit 15   Sport

Warm up

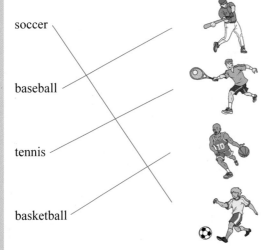

soccer

baseball

tennis

basketball

Reading

    A. 1. (A) 2. (B) 3. (B) 4. (B) 5. (D)

    B. 1. (C) 2. (B) 3. (A) 4. (B) 5. (C)

Vocabulary

    1. pitcher, hitter屬於人

    2. spherical, rectangular屬於形狀

    3. injury, tear, emergency, fatality 屬於傷害

Grammar

句型：

1. S +can + be + pp + to
2. S + try + to
3. S + be + to   +   原型動詞
4. S + be + pp. + to

    A. 1. (C) 2. (A) 3. (C) 4. (D) 5. (A)

Writing

    A. Answers may vary.

    B. Answers may vary.

    C. Answers may vary.

Speaking

    A. Search engine recommended: http://en.wikipedia.org/wiki/Main_Page

    B. Answers may vary

Listening

    A. 1. (A)   2. (A)   3. (B)   4. (C)

    B. 1. (B)   2. (C)   3. (D)   4. (C)

ESP

    A. 1. Stretch before and after sports training or games.

       2. Focus

       3. Strengthen the midsection

       4. Develop your self confidence

Unit 15   Audioscript

Track 34

Unit 15 Listening Part A. **Listen to the statements and choose the best answer.**

Today we're going to learn how to do breaststroke. The breaststroke includes two steps, your kick and your pull. Firstly, I would like to break down the kick into several parts. Within that kick, we need to bend the knees, open your legs, snap, and then glide. The glide lasts about two seconds. The next step is the pull. The pull includes four phases. You sweep outward first and next inward towards your chest, your recovery, and your glide. The final step is that you put your head down during the recovery. These simple steps can help you learn the breaststroke more easily.

Track 35

Unit 15 Listening Part B. **Listen to the statements and choose the best answer.**

Today we will learn how to do freestyle. When swimming freestyle, you should focus on the bottom line of the pool, keep your head down and allow your hips to float to the top. When taking each stroke, you should go ahead and let your body twist while keeping your head on the bottom. It is best to breathe every three strokes. So one, two, three, breathe, placing your ear on your shoulder and your cheek in the water. It's a five-step process, including the reach, the catch, the pull, the push, and the recovery. The last part of your free

Unit 16   Education

Warm up

Answers may vary

Reading

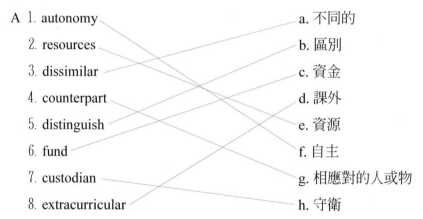

A 1. autonomy   a. 不同的
   2. resources   b. 區別
   3. dissimilar   c. 資金
   4. counterpart   d. 課外
   5. distinguish   e. 資源
   6. fund   f. 自主
   7. custodian   g. 相應對的人或物
   8. extracurricular   h. 守衛

Vocabulary

A. Answers may vary

Writing

A. Answers may vary.

B. Answers may vary.

Speaking

A. Answers may vary.

B. Answers may vary.

Listening

A.

What	When
The education reform evaluation committee was organized by the Executive Yuan	1994
The Executive Yuan organized an educational reform promotion team to work on implementing suggestions.	1996
The Educational Reform Action Program of the Ministry of Education (MOE) was approved by the Executive Yuan which provided a special budget of $5 billion US dollars.	1998

B. 1. (D)   2. (A)   3. (A)   4. (A)

ESP

C. Answers may vary

Unit 16 Audioscript

Unit 16 Listening Part A. **Listen to the following lecture and take notes.**

Ladies and gentlemen, it is a pleasure to have the opportunity to be here to speak to you, on behalf of Taiwan's Ministry of Education (MOE) about the current status of our educational reform movement. Taiwan has come a long way in transforming itself. The education reform evaluation committee was organized by the Executive Yuan in 199 4. During that time, educational reform has become a national topic of discussion. In 1996, the Executive Yuan organized an educational reform promotion team to work on implementing suggestions. The MOE then proposed a 12-point plan, which created a shift for Taiwan's educational transformation.

On May 14, 1998,the Educational Reform Action Program of the MOE was approved by the Executive Yuan which provided a special budget of $5 billion US dollars. This program pushed Taiwan forward into an "era of educational reform."

Unit 16 Listening Part B. **Listen to the following lecture and answer the questions.**

At an Executive Yuan meeting, the Ministry of Education presented a report on its "Technological and Vocational Education Reform Project - Expertise Training." This report aimed at improving the practical aspects of technological and vocational education and enhancing students' specialized skills. The implementation of this project will produce specialized workers who can meet job requirements and compete in related fields.

Technological and vocational education has already made significant contributions to the country because it has supplied the workforce for Taiwan's economic development and trained technical specialists for various levels. However, in order to face global competition and industrial transformation, technological and vocational education requires reexamination so as to improve both the content and methodology and to reform, innovate and improve the system on the existing foundation.

The objectives of this project include improving teaching and learning environments, bridging the gap between school teaching and industrial needs, and training specialists. The ultimate goals is to mold school teaching to meet the demands of industry in order to train students for the job market, increase their employment qualifications, and raise Taiwan's competitiveness.

國家圖書館出版品預行編目資料

Way to go:strategic approach to English learning
／黃聖慧總編著. 陳憶如、蔡佳蓉著
－－－版.－－臺北市：五南，2012.03
　面；　公分
參考書目：面
ISBN 978-957-11-6495-3 (平裝)
1.英語　2.讀本
805.18　　　　　　　　　　100024512

1X6K　英文系列

Way to go
strategic approach to English learning

總 編 審 — 黃聖慧(301.7)

作　　者 — 陳憶如、蔡佳蓉

發 行 人 — 楊榮川

總 編 輯 — 王翠華

主　　編 — 黃惠娟

責任編輯 — 胡天如

封面設計 — 黃聖文

版式設計 — 董子瑈

插　　畫 — 俞家燕

出 版 者 — 五南圖書出版股份有限公司

地　　址：106台北市大安區和平東路二段339號4樓

電　　話：(02)2705-5066　　傳　　真：(02)2706-6100

網　　址：http://www.wunan.com.tw

電子郵件：wunan@wunan.com.tw

劃撥帳號：01068953

戶　　名：五南圖書出版股份有限公司

台中市駐區辦公室/台中市中區中山路6號

電　　話：(04)2223-0891　　傳　　真：(04)2223-3549

高雄市駐區辦公室/高雄市新興區中山一路290號

電　　話：(07)2358-702　　傳　　真：(07)2350-236

法律顧問　元貞聯合法律事務所　張澤平律師

出版日期　2012年3月 初版一刷

定　　價　新臺幣350元